T0160763

The Lion's Share

A NOVEL BY ROCHELLE RATNER

Rochelle Ratner

COFFEE HOUSE PRESS :: MINNEAPOLIS :: 1991

Author acknowledgements: This novel would not have been possible without the generosity of numerous friends who offered editorial advice and encouragement, and who freely shared their knowledge of the New York City art world and corporate support of the arts. In particular, I'd like to thank Elizabeth Cook, Maurice Kenny, Allan Kornblum, Elizabeth Marraffino, Susan Mernit, Paul Pines, Corinne Robins and Bernie Solomon.

The publisher thanks the following organizations whose support helped make this book possible: Elmer L. and Eleanor J. Andersen Foundation; The Bush Foundation; Dayton Hudson Foundation; Jerome Foundation; Minnesota State Arts Board; the National Endowment for the Arts, a federal agency; and Northwest Area Foundation.

Coffee House Press books are distributed to the trade by Consortium Book Sales & Distribution, 287 E. Sixth St., Suite 365, St. Paul, Minnesota 55101. Our books are available through all major library distributors and jobbers, and through most small press distributors, including Bookpeople, Bookslinger, Inland, Pacific Pipeline, and Small Press Distribution. For personal orders, catalogs, or other information, write to:
COFFEE HOUSE PRESS
27 North Fourth Street, Suite 400, Minneapolis, MN 55401

Library of Congress Cataloging in Publication Data
Ratner, Rochelle.
    The lion's share : a novel / by Rochelle Ratner.
        p. cm.
    ISBN 0-918273-87-0 : $10.95
    I. Title.
PS3568.A76L5 1991
813'.54—dc20   91-24085
                                          CIP

9 8 7 6 5 4 3 2 1

CONTENTS

for Ken

CHAPTER ONE

Response to the Environment

TWO HEADS lay on the pillow, one of them a lion's. The other head stirred. Was it a siren? Jana opened her eyes, jolted upright, stared around the unfamiliar space until it became familiar once again: bed, window, chair, table, phone. Phone, yes, it was the phone; she'd been working late last night and must have forgotten to turn the ring off.

"Rise and shine," declared Jana's boss.

Even with the sleep in her eyes, Jana could see her watch: the date read March 21; the hands pointed to nine-thirty. Natalie knew damn well she usually slept till at least ten. "I can't find the floor plans for the Lincoln Center exhibit. They're not in either of the folders with the others," came the shrill voice through the phone.

"What?" Jana shook her curly brown hair to get the knots out. On close inspection, you could find one or two strands of gray.

"The Lincoln Center floor plans. I've looked all over the gallery. I can't find them anywhere."

"I brought them home Thursday night. I left a note on your desk."

"Well, it must have gotten buried in the rest of the clutter. What did you take them home for?"

"That underground arcade has so many tunnels and blind corners. I wanted to walk through on my own, without a dozen special-event co-ordinators leading me. I had to meet friends for brunch at The Ginger Man Saturday, so I was in the area. And I was right: we've been including at least thirty feet that are worthless for an exhibit, unless we're expecting an audience of ostriches and giraffes."

"Good thing you discovered it before we started mapping the installation. I'm sorry if I woke you. I panicked when I couldn't find the plans."

"When was the last time we lost anything?"

"There's always a first time." Natalie had been executive director of The Paperworks Space for eight years now. "You've no idea the kinds of problems I've had to deal with."

"So you've told me. Well, let me finish waking up." Jana hung up, crawled back under the flannel sheet, and hugged her lion to her. Leroy had been a birthday gift from Marilyn, her closest friend, three years ago last December when she'd turned thirty-one. Two months before that, they'd driven down to a Southern Graphics Association meeting in Virginia. Along the way they passed endless billboards advertising Jungle Wilderness, showing a boy proudly hugging a lion. Jana had fallen into her high-pitched little-girl voice, whining about wanting a lion to cuddle. It was only half in jest.

The conference had progressed exactly as expected. By the second day the "happily married" Marilyn was spending most of her free time with some guy she'd met. Virtuous Jana, on the other hand, attended strictly to business and wouldn't let herself be bothered with flirting. Not that the guys didn't try. There was one who helped her unlock her door the day it jammed, then stood there blocking her entrance, making small talk. There was the jerk from Atlanta who took her hand as he was showing her his prints; Jana quickly said she had a meeting in five minutes and ran off.

She didn't need men; there were plenty of other things to busy herself with. The first day she was on a panel discussing fundraising for the visual arts. The third day she gave a talk on curating shows in nonprofit spaces. There were continual lunch and dinner meetings with people on the association's board of directors. She made arrangements to look at the work of what seemed like a hundred different artists (five of whom they eventually showed), while running from meetings to cocktail parties and back again. But then, late at night, the queen-sized bed with its stark white sheets changed daily had accentuated her aloneness.

Sometimes those conferences reminded her of small towns, everyone knowing everyone, spending more time gossiping than working. She was at her worst in such situations. Even now, she sometimes imagined people could tell that she, a 34-year-old professional in the swinging art world, was still a virgin. It wasn't due to some hideous deformity. She might not be a beauty queen, but with her petite frame and naturally curly, shoulder-length brown hair, her appearance was moderately attractive. If that final moment never arrived in her occasional brief relationships with men, it was because she'd decided long ago that she didn't want it to. "Virginity—it isn't a disease," she said aloud, defensively.

She hugged Leroy closer to her, turned to face the wall. She had to keep reminding herself that she was a New Yorker: even virgins were lost in the crowd in a city this large. Anonymity was precisely what she'd been searching for when she'd moved to the city fifteen years ago. Neighbors smiled in the hall but never knocked on the door to sell Girl Scout cookies, they never asked in passing if she was "still painting."

Yes, she told herself again, she was a New Yorker, an artist. She rolled over, opened her eyes and, presto, everything within her field of vision offered confirmation: an easel and an old wooden drafting table (tilted at an angle that would be too sharp for anyone taller than five feet) stood back to back by the far window; beside them was the white plastic cart that held her paints (and had paint smudged on every conceivable surface, including the woman's head she'd painted on one corner years ago); the sheet of glass she used as a palette was laid on the counter, with racks of paintings beneath that; the floor space was easy to clear for larger works, the paint-stained linoleum covered uneven floorboards.

She pressed Leroy's plush body tight against her. It was disconcerting to realize she was the same person who, five or six years ago, had lain under these same sheets, in this same bed. The same person who had desperately needed to be painting every waking moment, as if it were the only way to justify her existence. She'd accomplished much in the past few years—a front page review in the art section of the *L.A. Times*, singled out by one New York critic two years ago as the best artist in a show at Nancy Hoffman's gallery . . .

And here she was on the verge of significant recognition as a curator. Associated Power and Light (or APL, pronounced Apple) pioneered in sponsoring art events throughout the city. They'd already provided backing for three shows at The Paperworks Space. But those shows were sidewalk art exhibits compared to the prospect of an exhibition in six public spaces, curated by The Paperworks Space, subsidized by APL: Artistic Response to the Environment. Given all the ecology issues getting attention these days, the concept seemed inspired. And the sites were all high-traffic areas: the underground arcade at Lincoln Center, the Central Park boat house, the Staten Island ferry terminal, the Mid-Manhattan Library, the second floor lobby at the World Trade Center, and the concourse at the Herald Center. To top it off, the budget included a forty-page catalog with eight pages of four-color-process reproductions, to be distributed free at selected locations.

Jana's mind was racing. No use going back to sleep now. She got up, put on her jeans and a flannel shirt, pulled her hair back and secured it with a rubber band, straightened the sheets. She picked the other animals off the floor and threw them on the bed any which way, yanked the Indian cotton bedspread off the window, and grabbed a cup of room-temperature coffee which had been sitting in the pot since yesterday. She turned on the radio and settled down to work on the painting which had kept her up till 3:00 AM. *Mulberry Street,* she called it: a buxom woman in a sleeveless house dress, graying hair uncombed, was leaning out a window, yelling to her children playing on the street. The children were little more than flat gray shadows, but in one corner of the painting lay a darker black form—the body of a twenty-four-year-old woman, raped and killed while walking home from work less than a year ago. The contrast between the violence of today and her memory of the city's innocence in 1969 disconcerted Jana, who usually avoided overt political statements.

This work speaks for more than the city, she reminded herself. Especially on a morning such as this, when she'd been harshly awakened by Nat's super-sweet voice, the painting seemed a memorial to her own earlier innocence. Her first apartment here had been on the corner of Mulberry and Grand streets, a four-room railroad flat she'd gotten for $150 a month. Jana recalled lugging canvases up the five flight walk-up, convinced that it was a temporary inconvenience—within two years she'd be making enough money off her art to hire an assistant to stretch canvases for her. Those were also the days when she assumed losing one's virginity was a magical rite that would take care of itself as soon as she was away from her parents' critical eyes. Talk about innocence...

The radio was blasting a commercial for Ronald Reagan—*Morning in America!* Snorting in disgust, Jana snapped the thing off. Deciding the painting before her was too drab, she mixed blue paint for the flowers in the woman's dress and emerged with an ungodly color. Her head was too foggy to concentrate. "Maybe it's wrong to pay too much attention to the past," she admonished herself.

But focusing on the present is even worse, she thought, glancing at her latest self-portrait propped against the far wall. While she had no intentions of becoming a modern-day Rembrandt, she was aware that she had to get closer to herself in order to sharpen her depiction of others. For the past three months she had, as an exercise, painted one self-portrait a week.

Did all short people really have no neck? No, of course she had a neck. She might be just under five feet tall, but she had a delicate bone structure, so the rest of her body was, as Marilyn would describe it, "cut to size." She didn't have that misshapen appearance she'd noticed in other short people. In this side view of her head and shoulders, she'd purposely depicted herself with her head down; on a painting two weeks ago, she'd let the neck show, and her mole turned into a dark blotch that jumped out at the viewer. I can never seem to get my hair color right, either, Jana realized. It might be a dull, indistinct brown, but the center of the curls always caught the light.

Trying to forget the face, she let her eyes move down the canvas. The upper half of her arms looked not only heavy, but flat, wide, more like her mother's than her own. On some supposed portrayals of herself, she'd ended up cluttering those arms with the liver spots she recalled on her mother's arms, a throwback to the time her mother had scarlet fever. On other portraits, she depicted huge sores from her own infected mosquito bites. Maybe it needs these awful blue flowers, Jana laughed, glancing back at *Mulberry Street.* No, she might not have perfect taste, but her clothes weren't *that* bad. Besides, those flowers were large, and the picture would appear top-heavy if she didn't show the whole upper half of her body.

All her self-portraits either stopped above the chest or began below it. Her frustrations concerning her breasts dated back to fifth grade, when she still wore an undershirt while the girls who'd grown breasts were being teased mercilessly by all the boys in the neighborhood, so she'd never gotten used to the idea of wearing this C cup. She refused to wear scarves or jewelry for similar reasons—they called attention to the top half of the body. "You just don't want to see yourself as interesting," Natalie said when Jana talked about these portraits. Maybe she was right. Even when painting someone she thought of as odd-looking, the finished work ended up gripping the viewer more than these self-portraits.

Telling herself she didn't have time to get caught up in self-analysis today, Jana grabbed the rolled-up Lincoln Center plans from her drafting table and laid them on the floor, put a stuffed animal on either end to keep them from rolling up again, and brooded. Were there any other hidden areas she'd overlooked? She knelt, examining that one narrow area, running charcoal over it to deepen the shading. What if APL insists they use every inch of available space? She'll argue that if they have to use that giraffe corner, at least put a painting there, something more colorful than the drawings selected for other places. Since it will be too late to find anything suitable from other artists, she'll have no choice but to hang *Mulberry Street.*

She picked up a sheet of plexiglass and quickly painted a thick black checkerboard pattern across it, then propped it in front of the painting to see the shading's effect—appalling. The figure appeared to be behind bars, trapped in the subway at Lincoln Center, not leaning out a tenement window. No matter where her paintngs were hung, the light seemed wrong.

Jana gave up, washed off the plexiglass, took a shower. She stuffed herself into gray slacks—a little too tight in the waist, but they were 100% wool and looked respectable. Then the black Danskin with the crew neck—out of fashion, she knew, but turtlenecks made her too hot. She put on the black satin jacket with the wine embroidery. . . no, too dressy. The black and green Chinese jacket? The sleeves were a little frayed. She settled on the gray tapestry jacket with the black fringe down the front, a dim reminder of how wrong that painting had looked. I look almost like the shadow of that murdered woman, Jana thought. I might not be able to paint self-portraits, but do I have to become my own haunting figures?

It was nearly twelve already. For someone who insisted she didn't give much thought to her appearance, she'd certainly wasted enough time dressing. She grabbed the floor plans, raced down the stairs, entered the subway just as a train was pulling in, and got to the gallery at five past one.

ℰ℘ ℰ℘

At five minutes past two, Jana Replansky and Natalie Connors were seated at the large oak conference table, making small talk with Frank Markowitz and his assistant, Marsha Tapscott. Ed Gabrielli, community coordinator in Associated Power and Light's Public Affairs division, stepped into the room.

"Sorry I'm late; I had some letters I wanted to look over and get out in this afternoon's mail," he explained, sliding into the nearest thickly cushioned chair. Promptness wasn't the only difference between Ed and his boss, Jana noted. Frank had a perfectly puffed handkerchief in the breast pocket of his jacket, its blue silk matching the jacket's lining perfectly. Ed had a pack of cigarettes casually jutting from that same pocket. Frank wore perfectly polished shoes; Ed wore Rockport DresSports— that's why his footsteps were so noticeably muffled by the room's charcoal carpet.

"Last week Ed audited a play we're sponsoring—he got to the theater in time for the final act," Frank said with an ironic smile. Ed winced at Frank's pathetic attempt at corporate humor, but he didn't sulk about it—he recognized the quip as Frank's device for getting the meeting underway. Papers were shuffled, chairs were pulled under the table. Jana clutched the floor plans, then glanced at Natalie, both wondering what surprises might await them, despite their thorough preparation for this meeting.

"Natalie," Frank began, "when you and Bill Fitch first ran this proposal by me last November, my response was enthusiastic. But the more I thought about it, the more concerned I was over the appropriateness of the sites you'd suggested and the security of the artwork. I must say, you've definitely allayed my concerns." As if to reiterate his statement, Frank let his hand rest on the presentation Natalie had sent him last month, with its detailed floor plans and accounts of other public exhibits and their security methods. As Frank looked over his notes, Ed shot a reassuring glance toward Natalie and Jana.

"After Ed, Marsha, and I considered the proposal and your budget in detail, however, we found ourselves facing other concerns. You list eighteen artists to be included in the exhibition, yet none of them have significant name recognition. We'd like to suggest that you include at least one well-known artist at each site."

"Well, The Paperworks Space mission statement declares that our purpose is to exhibit works on paper by artists who use paper as their major medium," Jana began. "The Artistic Response to the Environment exhibition might draw a wider audience by including well-known artists, but we want to be careful not to override our primary goal. If more established artists were included, we'd have to be extremely cautious in selecting them."

"When we present this proposal to our board, we could ask board members to suggest names and assist in any initial introductions," Frank offered.

"Instead of one well-known artist at each site, perhaps we could see our way clear to including two or three such artists," Natalie began, in a conciliatory tone. "Major artists might be appropriate at the more prominent locations, such as the World Trade Center or the Lincoln Center arcade. With careful artistic review, and with input from The Paperworks Space board, we should be able to select prominent artists whose work is appropriate."

Jana sucked in her breath. Well-known artists had enormous reservations about showing alongside those less established. Natalie's suggestion that the invitations come through The Paperworks Space board of directors might work, but someone on their board would have to be owed a lot of favors, and be willing to call them all in. Not to mention the favors they would, in turn, owe members of their board.

Frank jotted a few notes on his copy of the proposal. "When do you think you might be able to get back to us with artists whose names have the prestige we're looking for?" he asked.

Natalie glanced briefly at Jana shifting in her chair, then winged it. "We can assemble our list of names, contact the artists to determine their willingness to participate, and have biographical sketches in your hands in three weeks."

"If you can keep to that time schedule, we should have no problem getting the information to our board prior to their April meeting. Now, with regard to your budget," Frank continued, "you have allocated less than $5,000 for the opening reception. Assuming we fund the exhibition, we envision this as a far more elaborate affair." He suggested moving the ribbon-cutting ceremony to the World Trade Center and making it an evening cocktail party rather than a lunch-hour reception. "Then, why not follow up with a gala dinner dance at Windows on the World?"

Natalie, rapidly adding mental figures, felt her head begin to swim. The dinner dance Frank was proposing could easily cost more than they'd budgeted for the entire exhibition and would triple their administrative headaches. "We've budgeted for one additional temporary staff person to handle the extra work load, and several of our board members have promised to donate time to help with arrangements, but . . ."

"Why not consider dropping the gala from your budget and let our promotion department handle the affair?" Frank might have intended his smile to be reassuring, but Jana read it as patronizing, like his comment that APL could provide introductions to well-known artists. Obviously, he'd already discussed the prospect of taking over promo for the gala with Ed and Marsha; it seemed a fait accompli.

The next two hours seemed to fly, and before Natalie and Jana realized it the meeting was adjourned. Although Jana had been taken aback by the request for name artists and totally surprised at the proposal to turn the entire gala over to APL's promotion department, everything had gone well. A few other issues came up, but it seemed as if APL's foundation staff were behind the proposal. Of course the foundation staff didn't have the final power, but the board of directors usually went along with their recommendations.

Jana gave a small sigh and started packing up. Natalie shuffled the floor plan for the Staten Island ferry terminal from hand to hand, rolled it tightly, then passed it to Jana to put away. "Oh, I forgot to tell you. I have an appointment at the hairdresser at four-thirty," she announced.

"What?"

"I don't have time to get back to the gallery first. You can carry these downtown, can't you, Jana? My hairdresser's only a few blocks from here. It doesn't make any sense to go all the way downtown and then be late."

"Why didn't you tell me before?" Jana stopped packing and glared at Nat. Not only had they brought the floor plans, but they'd brought two portfolios of representative drawings on the off chance Frank would ask to see them.

"I didn't expect the meeting to last this late. I'm sorry."

Jana threw up her hands. "At least help me get a cab."

"Of course, of course. I won't abandon you." Jana heard steps behind her, then looked up to realize Ed had returned. In the few minutes since he'd left the room, he'd unbuttoned his jacket, making him appear less official. Jana found the sight of his slight potbelly more intimidating than the careful corporate demeanor.

"Let me give you a hand," he said, carefully rolling one of the plans before she could quite recover from her surprise.

"Oh great." Natalie's voice assumed that super-sweet tone again. "You can get her a cab, can't you? I'm late for another meeting. Jana, I'll see you tomorrow morning." And she was gone.

"I wonder if you can manage these." Ed ran his fingers through hair that had gone pure white nearly two decades ago, before he'd turned twenty-five.

"I'll manage," Jana said. Then, laughing nervously, she added, "I'm used to lugging canvases around." She had to admit that Ed's sturdy frame was better suited to carrying the portfolios. He probably wasn't more than five-foot-seven or -eight, but next to Jana he seemed gigantic. "It's only these plush offices that make me feel so small," she told herself. The entire annual budget of The Paperworks Space probably didn't come close to the cost of the furnishings in one of APL's five conference rooms.

"I have my car around the corner. If you can wait twenty minutes until I straighten up some things in my office, I'll drive you downtown," Ed said. Then, catching her confused reaction, he tried to explain himself: "I don't usually drive to work, but I was running late this morning, and impulsively decided I wanted the car. Who knows, maybe I even suspected a damsel in distress," he laughed.

Jana smiled agreement. A ride downtown would give her a chance to smooth over the scene Ed witnessed. She didn't want APL to get the wrong impression about her working relationship with Natalie; an incident like this might come up once every six months, but generally they made a good team. She watched him walk down the corridor toward his office, strutting like a peacock. She didn't like being thought of as a "damsel in distress," and that stride made her wonder if Ed had been scheming a way to be with her all along. "More than likely, he was thinking about Natalie," she consoled herself. Choosing attractive friends, like Natalie and Marilyn, was another way in which Jana protected herself against the threat of romantic involvement.

૯/૭ ૯/૭

Ed called the garage, which had his dark green Toyota waiting when they got there. Jana noticed that it was in good shape for a six- or seven-year-old car. As a kid, her father played a game with her, asking her to guess the make and year of every car they passed. In the early fifties they were easier to distinguish.

Ed opened the passenger door for her, reaching for her arm to help her into the car. She thrust the portfolios toward him, and he accepted them with one hand while placing his free arm around her. Jana froze. Here we go again, she thought; it might be a different man, but I have the same reaction. She didn't have the nerve to jerk away. As she stood there it felt as if Ed were pressing one finger, then another, then his entire hand, against her shivering flesh. At first his hand seemed to be all bony knuckles, then she stopped feeling anything, only the pressure, the presence of him next to her. Much heavier than those portfolios would have been. Dead weight.

At last he stepped aside and let her in, then walked around to the driver's side. He pushed his way onto the heavily trafficked street the way cabbies did, making the other cars stop and wait for him, while Jana stared out the window, hating this silence. At meetings there was always business to discuss, five or six people with which to make small talk during breaks. Natalie had a talent for small talk. Jana should have remembered how difficult it was for her to relate casually to men; she should have realized she'd be at a loss for words on her own like this.

The one other time she'd met Ed, at a meeting last month, he'd asked if she were an artist as well as a curator. When she'd told him yes, he'd asked whether her drawings would be included in the exhibition. "I work on paintings, large works," she'd told him. And Ed had suggested maybe she'd *want* to do some drawings, since the exhibition was still over a year off. She countered with a brief monologue on the etiquette involved in entering one's own work in a show one was curating, but felt as if only the plush chairs were listening. Ed also mentioned wanting to see her paintings sometime. He'd probably ask her to "explain" them, she thought, turning her attention to the heavy rush hour traffic.

She leaned back and tried to relax. The bright sun, reflected off the windows of buildings, made its patterns in her hair. She'd washed it two days ago, so it was all frizzy now, blowing across her forehead, adding to her discomfort. When she'd gone away to camp as a kid, the girls in her bunk were divided into two groups. One group washed their hair on Sundays, the other group on Wednesdays. On Sunday, when Group A washed, she would always claim she'd been put in Group B. When Wednesday came around, she would insist she was in Group A and had just washed. She might have been caught, but she was in the infirmary half the Wednesdays and Sundays anyway. That doctor never seemed to mind, or even notice how dirty her hair was. He'd just lain her there on his cot, not really looking at her . . . Putting her attention to better use, she wondered if those awful camp memories were part of the reason she never captured her hair in self-portraits.

Ed rounded the corner onto Prince Street. Jana sat up straight, twirled two fingers through her hair to encourage its ringlet curl, and stiffly uncrossed her legs. Time to become professional again, time to give the gentleman from APL the grand tour of the gallery. Come on, she kept telling herself, put on one of those bright phony smiles you always use for corporate executives and art critics. She'd had a difficult time with that smile, at first—it seemed pretentious, so far from what made art real for her. But she knew it was important, and much as she hated to admit it, she'd become good at it. Pretend Ed's John Perreault or Peggy Guggenheim, she told herself again. Peggy Guggenheim would have been a cinch. She opened and closed the clasp on her pocketbook, suddenly envious of women who used makeup and had compacts to glance into at times like this.

Ed found a parking space and she hopped out of the car, accidentally slamming the door. She was fumbling with her keys by the time Ed had gotten the portfolios out of the back. Natalie teased her about weighing her huge pocketbook down with as many keys as a janitor—apparently it wasn't sexy for women to carry a lot of keys around.

"Welcome to The Paperworks Space, Main Gallery," she said as she switched on the lights. In her nervousness, she'd momentarily forgotten that Ed had been here for a meeting, shortly after the exhibition was first proposed. "Welcome back, rather," she corrected herself.

Taking one of the descriptive brochures from the window ledge, she held it in front of her face and pretended to check it over before handing it to Ed. "This contains a statement by Lou Daniels, the artist whose drawings are in this room," she said. "You might recall discussing him at our last meeting. He's the young rebel graphic artist from San Francisco—this is his first show on the East Coast. Natalie and I are especially excited about introducing him to a wide, general audience through the Artistic Response to the Environment exhibit."

Talking quickly, she told him about the artist on exhibition in the two smaller rooms. "If you'll excuse me for a moment, I'll go in the back and get a copy of his promo sheet and price list. There have been more people than usual through here the past few days, and the stack seems to have evaporated." The exhibition space occupied 1,500 square feet, and Jana was grateful for every blessed inch of it. She let Ed look around alone, taking longer than necessary to gather the information she needed. By the time he'd finished looking at Lou's work, she was able to thrust the vitae on the other artist into his hands and busy herself with paperwork at her desk.

Out of the corner of her eye, she watched Ed survey Lou Daniels' work from room-center, then begin a closer inspection. Even from behind, she could tell his reaction was the same as that of others seeing Lou's work for the first time. Initially his drawings appear to be architectural blueprints, pencil lines on grid paper. Then it would dawn on the viewer that these blueprints weren't for buildings; they were for landscapes, with plans for trees, birds, bushes, broken fences. The one Ed was studying now included wind circling one tree and shadows running off the left side of the page.

His interest in the drawings reassured Jana that she'd been making too much of his attentiveness to her in the car. "I'll bet he's envisioning Lou's work fitting into APL's concept of the Artistic Response to the Environment exhibition," Jana guessed. Even though she'd described the artist as a "rebel," these drawings didn't shock or offend; there were no nuclear explosions, no radioactive waste dumps. Their original exhibition proposal had included five pages of biographical material about the artists they planned to include, carefully outlining the content of their work and conveying to APL the message that overtly provocative imagery would be carefully avoided, but Jana was delighted to see Ed further reassured by this walk-through.

He took a quick look at the smaller rooms, then eased his way over to Jana's desk. "I'm impressed," he said.

"Well, that's good."

"Which of these two artists do you prefer? Give me your personal opinion."

But this wasn't a personal visit: he was a grants officer for a major corporation, and she wanted to keep a professional veneer to the conversation. "I like them both, but for different reasons." Jana barely looked up from her papers, for a moment feeling out of place in her own gallery. She shifted her pen from one hand to the other. Ed patiently waited for her to continue. "Lou's work features a minutely detailed exploration of space. His concentration on depth and perspective makes him perfect for the Central Park boat house, where the windows will add a further dimension. I've overheard viewers comment that they want to crawl inside some of his mazes and wander around in them." To be honest, she found his drawings cold and intellectual, but it was easier for her to talk shop than to think about being alone in the gallery with a man.

"We have some brochures around from Lou's other shows, if you want me to hunt for them," she continued, getting to her feet as she was talking. "A review appeared in the San Francisco Chronicle that I found extremely perceptive." Lou Daniels was better than most of the artists who exhibited in this gallery, artists with no sense of direction, wanting nothing more than to blend in with the crowd, paint or draw highly salable imitations of what everyone else was drawing. Well, she would have done that if she could have, especially when she'd first moved to the city, she reminded herself. She'd never studied art per se, never mastered the techniques of imitation—a blessing in disguise.

"No, no, don't bother searching for more material." Ed was anxious not to lose her under more papers. "You've done a more than adequate job of explaining his process." He stared for a moment at the distant back walls of the gallery.

Oh Christ, Jana thought. I shouldn't have gone on so long about Lou's work. I'll bet he's wondering if I pull away when Lou touches my arm. "Yes!" she wanted to scream, "Yes, yes, yes! I pull away from *all* men!"

Ed turned and looked out the huge front windows at the street. "As we were driving here, I was noticing how much the neighborhood has changed," he began. "I wouldn't mind walking around and exploring a bit. Do you feel like joining me, maybe showing me your favorite places? We could stop for a drink or even dinner..."

"Thanks, but I've got things to finish up here," Jana said, barely looking at him.

"Okay, we'll make it some other time." This was going to be tricky, he thought. A business lunch to discuss a proposal was one thing, but driving down here he'd begun to realize that his interest in Jana Replansky might go beyond the bounds of his professional responsibilities. He didn't want Jana to think she had to socialize with him in order to guarantee funding for the proposal, but he understood she might have interpreted his invitation that way. He suddenly felt top-heavy, unsure about the best way to exit gracefully. "I'll see you soon," he said, as he reached out to awkwardly shake her hand.

Jana shuffled through a pile of papers, letting Ed find his own way out. She found herself thinking about Ed's bald spot. She'd never noticed it before, but as he'd walked out, she'd spotted the classic half-dozen hairs combed carefully over a balding pate. Staring at one of the postcards announcing Lou Daniels' show, she picked up a pen and wrote in *bald spot.* A vast improvement. Lou's work would grow enormously if he could open up, let particulars about people enter his landscapes. He seemed right on the verge of doing that. A year from now, five years from now, there was no telling where he'd be. In one of the larger galleries, more than likely.

She dropped the postcard into the wastebasket. Thinking about Lou's work was supposed to take her mind off Ed, but no such luck. Was she going to go home and draw bald spots on grid paper? Damn Ed. Damn all the artists who seemed to be clouding her own vision.

No, the artists were no problem; damn all the *men* who seemed to be clouding her vision. Truth was, she'd been thinking about Ed since their first meeting. She remembered wanting him to like her immediately. It was almost a sexual, or at least sensual, feeling. She hadn't expected Ed's touch to remind her of her sexual bald spots. She thought she'd matured since she'd moved to the city fifteen years ago, that she'd be able to handle a relationship now, but her growth was all in her mind. Her body still remembered the way things used to be, and reacted according to conditioning. She would have frozen at the touch of any male hand.

She glanced at her watch and saw ten minutes had passed. That should be long enough for Ed to have gotten to his car and driven off, or at least to have walked a few blocks away, if he actually did decide to explore the area. She made a quick tour around the gallery, following the same route he'd taken. When she'd first begun working here, they had often had concurrent shows by as many as four artists, and were able to present each piece appropriately. But drawings didn't take up the room paintings did, they didn't present nearly as many problems with hanging, or lighting. Regardless of what the gallery's mission statement said, in her own art she viewed drawings as preludes to larger works.

She locked up and treated herself to a cab uptown, deciding to pay herself back from petty cash. She was anxious to be alone in her own apartment—maybe she'd curl up in bed and read a while. She picked up a ham sandwich at the corner bodega; she couldn't deal with stopping in a coffee shop tonight. By seven o'clock she was undressed. It was too warm for flannel pajamas, especially pajamas with feet, but she put them on anyway, watching in dismay as her big toes poked through the soles. She'd looked all over town to find these and didn't relish the prospect of shopping for new ones, hurrying past the cosmetic counter at Bloomingdale's before they sprayed her with perfume.

She left all the animals on the bed and positioned herself among them, propping her head on the turtle's back. She took two bites of a sandwich and found herself wondering what her parents were eating. Marilyn had said years ago that Jana's difficulties in relating to men most likely had something to do with her parents. "Maybe you felt excluded from their sexual relationship," Marilyn suggested. Jana had rejected that theory; it was hard to think of her parents as being sexual creatures, all but impossible to imagine them in bed together. "If you must know, it probably has more to do with a seventy-year-old doctor I met when I was away at summer camp," Jana might have answered, but that wasn't an experience she could talk about, even with Marilyn.

She tossed the other animals off the bed, clung tight to Leroy, and picked up a book. Leroy had been the first in her collection of stuffed animals, and he was still her favorite; the others were smaller, less cuddly. She lay back, the three-foot lion almost as big as her own body, his front legs crossed on her chest, one back leg soft and warm between her thighs. Keeping her arms at her sides, she twisted a corner of the sheet between her fingers. "Never tell anyone about how we do this," she whispered in his plush ear. "It will be our secret."

CHAPTER TWO

The Last Meeting

"Too bad Ed is a grants officer, instead of a member of the panel that approves the grants," Natalie muttered the next day. "We'd have it made."

"What makes you say that?" Jana asked, staring at an enormous stack of papers Nat had left on her desk that morning.

"I think he likes you."

"What? Don't be ridiculous."

"He offered you a ride back here, didn't he?"

"He was just being helpful. He said he had to see someone downtown," Jana lied.

"Ed is a corporation man—he can't spare time to be 'helpful.' He *likes* you."

"It was nothing more than a friendly gesture. He's considerate."

"Why do you immediately dismiss the idea that a guy might be interested in you?"

"I don't know if he's interested or not; I don't always pick up those signals. But if The Paperworks Space is depending on me to sleep our way to grant money, then we're in big trouble," Jana said in her usual effort to joke about her virginity.

Natalie wasn't laughing. She walked over to Jana's desk, positioning herself directly in front. "That's not the point. What I'm trying to say is that you can't continue running away from men. Ed's not an artist—maybe that will help you to relax and be yourself with him."

"That's ridiculous," Jana mumbled.

"No it's not. Your figure's almost as good as it was when we first met, if you spruced yourself up a bit, you could look every bit the femme fatale. You don't have to make a huge effort—you could just get some colorful scarves, maybe a gold bangle. Even if Ed's only casually interested, I bet he'd totally flip next time he sees you."

"When we first met . . ." Jana muttered, remembering. Fifteen years ago Natalie had been twenty-eight, newly divorced, and into her earthmother role. It seemed natural for her to befriend Jana, a timid kid two years out of high school she'd met in a painting class. One Saturday when she had nothing better to do, she called Jana and suggested they meet for lunch. Later they went back to her place, and she spent an hour painting Jana's face. The makeup made her feel like a clown, but in those days Jana was willing to accept anything Nat said as gospel: she was older and more familiar with the art world. Now they were equals, professionally, but Natalie's determination to "cure" her virginity continued to rankle. Sometimes Jana could let Natalie's stream of advice rush over her head, but this wasn't one of those times.

"Why don't you get your hair done?" Natalie continued. "Or better yet, let me set it for you. We can do it tonight. We'll go shopping, grab some dinner, come back to my place, and I'll fix your hair."

"Nat, please. I appreciate all you're trying to do, but I'm simply not interested."

Not quite pouting, but with all the excitement drained out of her, Natalie settled in at her desk. She looked up some numbers in the Rolodex, made a few notes on scrap paper. She got up and sharpened her pencil. "Are you certain you want to spend the rest of your life alone?" she asked, stopping at Jana's desk on her way back. When Jana didn't respond, she continued probing: "You seem confused lately. I've watched your reactions when people come into the gallery. If you see a couple hugging or flirting, your whole body tightens up. I think you're jealous."

"Maybe I am jealous, but it's not rational."

"Rational?" Natalie scoffed, then unloaded a little bomb. "I bet if you got involved with someone it would help your painting." She took a step back and turned away, allowing the statement its full effect.

Jana glanced at Natalie towering over her, then realized she no longer cared about anything her friend thought might "help her painting." Nat had become too much of an administrator, looking only at the finished works; she was no longer close to the artistic process. "I hope I never get to that point," Jana told herself. Until now, working at The Paperworks Space had prevented her from forming distorted impressions. She was convinced that working in a situation where she was forced to judge art, to separate potential from mediocrity, had forced her to look at her own painting more critically as well.

And painting was still her main focus. Fifteen years ago, it had been the nucleus of her friendships. It was what solidified her bonds with both Natalie and Marilyn. People were expected to change, but still . . . Natalie had never been the most dedicated painter in the world, but these days she'd given up the pretense of having a canvas always stretched and ready. And Marilyn, whose commitment to her work used to be an inspiration to Jana, had spent the better part of the past ten years on textile design. Marilyn's interest in textiles had begun as a way to make extra money when she was pregnant; "domesticating myself," she'd jokingly called it. Then, staying home with the baby, she looked around the apartment and became more aware of fabrics interacting in her life. As much as Marilyn might insist that her painting had always been rooted in design and this medium offered just as much opportunity for self-expression, Jana could see through that guise. She had to protect herself against such drastic changes; it was her single-minded attention to painting which had kept her so clearly on the same course all these years. All the more reason not to think too much about Ed, or any other man.

She let her eyes as well as her thoughts wander, trying to decide how to end this conversation with Natalie without one of them getting upset. She chewed on the eraser of her pencil the way she'd done as a kid, then tapped the wet tip on the desk. Directly in front of her, the Rolodex was open to Bill Fitch, president of the gallery's board of directors. "We're not going to get any calls made if we stand around here talking all afternoon," Jana said. "We promised Frank we'd speak to our board and get back to him with suggestions for prominent artists to include in the exhibition. I purposely came in early today to get started on that."

"They'll come up with someone," Nat mumbled. She was no more anxious than Jana to play phone tag with their board members, presenting this compromise with APL as a successful negotiation, then asking them to call in all their favors.

"I'm glad one of us has confidence in our board," Jana said. "We've never asked for anything like this before."

"We selected our board members because of their influence and connections. A situation like this is precisely what they're there for." They both picked up phones and started dialing.

ᑲ ᑲ

Jana called Larry Rivers, whom they'd added to their board last year because of his connections in the international art world. At first Larry seemed reluctant to help but finally agreed to speak with a young artist who'd been included in the Whitney Biennial for the past several years, and whose recent shows in New York had gotten widespread attention. He was an Abstract Expressionist who used handmade paper as his medium, "drawing" by molding the still-wet pulp. It was stretching the issue to consider his "landscapes" environmental commentary, but Jana wasn't in a position to quibble. "He apprenticed with me ten years ago," Larry said. "I was the one who introduced him to galleries in Germany and Switzerland. If it hadn't been for those shows, his work wouldn't have been readily accepted by the New York art scene. We've stayed on friendly terms—I have a feeling he'll do anything to keep it that way."

Natalie spoke with Bill. As one of the top vice presidents at Nationbank, as well as an art patron, he had engineered Nationbank's purchase of several large paintings over the past ten years. If anyone on their board was owed favors, it would be Bill. And as board president, he'd gone with Natalie the first time she'd presented the proposal to APL, so he was more involved in this project than the other board members. He'd see it as his responsibility to come up with a renowned artist who'd be willing to participate.

A cautious person who thought things over carefully, then spoke with what bordered on a southern drawl, Bill took even longer than usual to reply to her request. And when she heard his response, she understood his caution. "I don't suppose Matt Fillmore would be appropriate, would he?" Bill asked.

Matt Fillmore was one of the last names Natalie had expected. "Well, he does use drawing as his major medium," she said. "And it would be an understatement to say that his work's environmentally concerned." She'd seen a show of his last fall, and two drawings stood out in her mind. One depicted a road race being run at Three Mile Island, the other showed garbage floating along the Hudson next to the Circle Dayliner. "Do you think he'd be willing to let us include his work?"

"I suspect so," Bill said. "He's a friend of my wife's brother, and I've known him socially for many years. It was through my instigation that he got the mural commission for Nationbank's Dallas headquarters two years ago, so it also wouldn't be the first time his work has had corporate backing."

"In other words, you think he knows how far he can push a sponsor?"

"I think he'll make direct statements about obvious trouble spots, but for the most part his work offers subtler commentary."

"Unfortunately, it's the trouble spots that stick out in my mind," Natalie said. "Those are also his strongest pieces."

"The question is: are there any trouble spots in APL's recent past?"

"Not that I can think of."

"I can't recall any, either. APL uses nuclear power, of course. The general public doesn't realize it, but large cities wouldn't be able to function without some forms of nuclear energy. But I don't recall them having any accidents or near misses."

"Let's just hope it stays that way," Natalie said. When Bill asked if she wanted a few days to think it over, she jumped at the chance. Not that there was much to think about—Matt Fillmore was probably the most appropriate artist around—but the more people she could draw into making this final decision, the less the burden would rest on her shoulders. And Jana was curator, after all; it should be her decision.

"I guess we don't have much choice, do we?" Jana stated more than asked. "We knew when we first talked about a show of environmentally concerned art that we might be dealing with some heavy issues, and the board agreed with us that it was important, right?" They waited two days, and spoke to the other board members. They threw Matt's name out, and everyone's reaction was pretty much the same as Bill's had been: his work's certainly appropriate; let's hope for the best. No one came up with a better suggestion.

Bill spoke with Matt Fillmore, then had Jana call and give him the particulars. "He seems like an easy-going guy," Jana said out loud as she put the phone down. Larry Rivers called on Thursday afternoon to say the artist he'd suggested was willing to participate. Natalie thought she was being optimistic by promising to get back to APL with the names of these artists in three weeks; as it turned out, they had all the material together, including bios and letters of interest from the artists, by the end of the following week, and they arranged a meeting for the following Thursday. "This ought to be the last meeting with Frank, Ed, and Marsha," Natalie prayed, delicately crossing her fingers. "After this it will be up to APL's board of directors."

Natalie had appointments in midtown on Thursday morning. She wanted to go over the bios with Jana before the meeting, to double-check which aspects of these artists they should stress, so they met in a little coffee shop around the corner from the APL building. They were standing in the short line, waiting to be seated, when Ed walked in, alone. Before Jana could catch her breath and smile, she heard Natalie inviting him to join them. For a moment Jana wondered if Nat had planned this accidental meeting, then decided it wasn't possible. Her boss might be a hopeless romantic, but she also had innate business sense; when contradictory aspects of her personality came into conflict, the level-headed executive won out.

Jana stared at the white tile wall their table was set against. This place looked more like a bathroom than a coffee shop, and sorely lacked the individuality one found in coffee shops in Soho or the Upper East Side. She raised her fork and watched the tile catch its reflection. Ed, sitting across from them, seemed to be going out of his way to talk with Natalie, telling her how much he'd enjoyed touring the gallery, asking questions about individual drawings. Jana was beginning to think maybe she and Nat *had* misinterpreted Ed's romantic interests.

She looked across the table to catch Ed rubbing his eye, trying to push a contact lens back in place. "Excuse me," he said to no one in particular. He left the table and headed for the men's room.

"Get it fixed?" Jana asked when he came back.

"For the moment, at least. Once those things start moving around in my eye, I'm usually in for a full day of trouble."

"Ever lose one?"

"No, but I've ripped them. I did that the first week I had them."

"That's the sort of thing I'd probably do."

"Before I got them, all my friends were telling me how wonderful soft lenses were. Now all I hear are their horror stories."

"I'll bet. I'd be terrified at the thought of putting something in my eye. Besides, I like having my glasses as a shield." Small, gold granny glasses; she'd worn them long before they were considered fashionable.

"As do I," Ed laughed. "I've never broken the habit of pushing my glasses up on my nose when I'm absorbed in thought, even though they're no longer there."

They finished the meal in silence, but it was an easy silence, miles away from the tension that had filled the car two weeks ago. Soon plates were pushed aside; Ed stubbed out his Camel in a flimsy tin ashtray. He ground the butt into the tin, anxious to catch every last spark. Jana glanced at the potato chips left on his plate.

Ed noticed. "Help yourself," he said, pushing the plate toward her. "But I warn you, one potato chip has twelve calories. I keep close track." He stood up and playfully tightened his belt a notch.

Jana took one chip. She had her hand halfway toward a second, then pulled back and pretended to hunt around in her purse for something. If they didn't get out of here soon, they'd be late for the meeting.

৫/১ ৫/১

The meeting itself took less time than lunch had taken. Frank got right down to business, so pleased with the luster these new artists would bring to the exhibit that he seemed to overlook Matt Fillmore's highly charged political stance. He probably knows the name but not the work, Jana realized.

"Between your proposal and the biographical profiles of these artists, I think we have a solid game plan to take to the board," he said. "Our board meeting is scheduled for Monday, April 18, and we should be able to let you know their decision shortly after that. If you don't hear from us by the following Friday, give Ed a call."

Ed lingered for a moment after Frank left, as if to reestablish personal contact. He told the two women that, assuming the proposal went through, the funds would be disbursed in two payments. "It takes roughly a week to get the paperwork out once the decision's been made, but we can cut the first check fairly quickly if you need money to get things underway." He smiled as if the proposal were through already.

By two o'clock Jana and Natalie were in a cab headed downtown, celebrating their success. Natalie returned to her favorite theme of late: "I think you and Ed make a cute couple."

Jana mumbled something about Natalie needing her head examined.

"He managed to get your address, didn't he?" Natalie's words would echo in Jana's ear for the next three weeks, drowning out thoughts of APL's board meeting. It was true: before they had left the coffee shop Ed mentioned that he was going up to Maine for a vacation and wanted to make sure he had their addresses so he could send postcards.

ॐ ॐ

Ed called on Wednesday, one of Jana's days off, to tell Natalie the funding had been approved, adding that he was taking off in two days and promising to put the paperwork in motion before he left town.

Unfortunately he was not as efficient in his personal life; Jana never received the card he'd promised. The adventurous part of her hoped to hear from him, while the workaholic was relieved. Just when she'd concluded that his interest was purely professional, Ed called her at home — he obviously still had her number, although he claimed he'd lost his address book (his excuse for not writing).

His trip had gone smoothly, he told her. It was too early for the tourists, so the rooms were cheaper, and the vacation itself was restful. He talked about Maine's ragged coastline, claiming he'd never seen anything like it: driving along Route 1, one minute you're following the beach, the next minute you're ten miles inland. He told her about side trips he'd made to various islands. "One night I stayed on an island whose only structure was an old stone mansion converted into a rooming house. You could walk across a thin wooden bridge to another island that was all rocky, deserted beach. I woke up the next morning and could have sworn I saw haystacks out the window. Turned out it was seaweed, gold and still wet, left on the rocks at high tide."

"Popping seaweed was one of the few aspects of the beach I enjoyed when I was growing up," Jana said. "It was never piled up like haystacks, though, just strands scattered about. I used to think they resembled branches, and before I popped them I spread them out on the sand in different gnarled tree-trunk patterns."

"You would have enjoyed hunting for driftwood along the Maine coast, then. The pieces were beautifully shaped, washed smooth by the waves. I brought home one piece that I swore at first was the bone of a rat or some other small animal. You'll have to see it."

"Jersey beaches never had much in the way of driftwood. Plenty of shells, though. Most of them were broken, but even the broken shapes made fascinating patterns. I could have stared at those shells for hours."

"Were you one of those kids who painted clam shells and sold them as ash trays?" Ed asked jokingly.

"Not on your life. I never wanted to interfere with their natural iridescence."

"That's how I feel about coral. When I was a kid, we used to go to Miami every Christmas to visit my grandparents, and I remember being enchanted by the pieces of coral along the beach."

"Unfortunately Lakewood didn't have much in the way of coral, either. But I've seen its beauty. I have friends who went to Florida especially to collect coral to use for their bathroom floor."

"What a great idea. It sounds gorgeous." Then, changing the subject a bit, he asked how her three weeks had been.

She told him they'd been hectic. "I'm going up to Yaddo a week from Friday, and I'm trying to get a thousand things done before I leave."

"You're going where?"

"Yaddo. It's an artists' retreat in Saratoga Springs. An invitation is considered an honor, and this is the third time they've invited me." She didn't bother mentioning that she'd been rejected the first two times she applied, and how devastated she'd been. That had been back in the early seventies, when she didn't need the time for uninterrupted work as much as she wanted the connections to be made at colonies such as Yaddo or MacDowell. Despite recommendations, Yaddo rejected her twice, MacDowell three times. She might have wanted time out of the city, but she was too proud to apply to the less prestigious colonies such as Cummington or Virginia Center for the Creative Arts. All or nothing, no compromises—that's the way she'd always been, but only in the past five or six years had it paid off for her.

"I didn't realize you were leaving town," Ed said after a moment's silence. "For a few weeks?"

"A few months. Unless unforeseen problems arise, I'll be up there till early September."

"How are you able to get that much time away from The Paperworks Space?" He'd hoped this call would help him get to know Jana better, and at first that seemed to be happening. But hearing she was leaving

town came as a disappointment. Quickly the little businessman inside
him took over, and he began to question the professionalism of the people running the project he'd just recommended for a considerable
amount of funding.

"I'm the artistic director, the curator. Natalie's the executive director," Jana reminded him. "She'll keep the doors open till June 15. Then
we're open by appointment only through Labor Day."

"What about the artists you're exhibiting?"

"We don't offer shows during the summer. Not many people walk the
streets doing the gallery tour when it's hot out, and certainly anyone who
can afford it gets out of the city. Nat tried staying open through July a few
years ago, and I think she sold two drawings the entire month. Most
New York galleries close for the summer."

"I guess I've been working too hard to notice," Ed laughed, trying to
ease his way back to the original purpose of his call. He explained that in
his position as community coordinator he reviewed a wide range of proposals from organizations throughout the metropolitan area, but most
of the proposals from arts associations had been given to Marsha for review. The closest he'd come to working on an arts project before theirs
had involved booking conservationists onto talk shows and monitoring
the programs APL sponsored on WNET. Jana's familiarity with the art
world was one of the traits which sparked his interest, he realized now.
"Do you have time to get together for a drink before you leave town?" he
asked.

Jana pressed the receiver tight against her cheek. She wanted very
much to see him. But she was also suddenly frightened of seeing him
alone again, without Natalie, without the pretense of a business meeting. "Can we leave it up in the air?" she asked. "I want to see how packing
and last-minute tasks go."

"We can do anything," Ed said.

Silently Jana repeated his words, changing the pronoun: I can do anything I set my mind to, she told herself. If she met him for a drink Thursday
night, she'd have ten days to psyche herself up for it. "Maybe Thursday
night..." she said out loud.

"Why don't I give you a call Thursday night, and we'll play it by ear?"

"Great," Jana said. "But don't tie yourself down if other things come
up," she added. "As I said, I don't know for sure if I'll have time. Too

often I find myself leaving things for the last minute. I've got clothes to pack, and painting supplies. I have to run down to Pearl Paint and buy some extra brushes and sketchbooks. I never find time to draw in the city anymore; that's one of the things I'm looking forward to this summer." Think about art, not about Ed, she chanted under her breath. It'll make seeing Ed easier.

"Hopefully you'll get everything accomplished in plenty of time. It would be good to see you."

It would be good to see you, too, Jana thought but didn't say, praying she could psyche herself up for it.

"I'll talk to you on Thursday night," Ed said again.

Jana impulsively picked up all her stuffed animals and shoved them into the back of a closet. It was to be her last energetic act before leaving town. She packed absentmindedly, spent hours on end mooning around the gallery. Over the next week and a half, she often caught herself studying the relationships of just about everyone she came into contact with, trying to see where she and Ed might fit in this paired-off scheme of things. In one fantasy, they had already moved in together, and she was trying to find a way to break the news to her parents.

სი სი

Thursday night Jana sat in her apartment, packed, waiting for Ed to call, fearing he wouldn't. Finally, a few minutes after nine, he called, and they decided to meet at her place. "It's 342 East 95th Street, Apartment Seven—second floor rear," she said, not wanting to say something stupid like "it will be good to see you," but feeling she had to say something. She hung up the phone and went right back to sitting and waiting. Then, when he walked in the door, the first thing he did was hug her. She stood on tiptoes to kiss him, and narrowly missed coming down on his foot. An elbow jabbed her waist. From that point on, the evening seemed to go straight downhill.

Since they were on the Upper East Side, Ed suggested they walk over to Elaine's for a drink—he'd heard it was a place many writers and artists hung out. Jana claimed it was too noisy. She was interested in producing art, not in being noticed around the art world, the way Ed suddenly seemed to be. She suggested a little cafe around the corner which had outside tables.

The place had only six tables outside, but people were leaving one. She ordered wine and Ed ordered a gin and tonic, only to be told they served nothing stronger than wine and beer. Making the best of it, he asked what they had on draft. They only had bottled beer. He settled for Heineken, insisting he didn't mind, his body tense, fidgeting. He fumbled around for a few minutes, tapping a cigarette on the ashtray, before he smiled and asked Jana where she'd gone to school.

"Does high school count? Woodrow Wilson High in Lakewood, New Jersey." She tried her best to toss off her answer as if it was nothing important. She was improving: a few years ago she would have felt insecure about her credentials and made up some college. Tonight she didn't even bother to mention she'd studied with Francis Harriman at The New School when she'd first moved to New York. More than "studied with him"; for two years she'd been his prize student. Here was a guy who, others said, taught women with his prick, yet he'd taken her seriously as an artist.

"You're kidding," Ed interrupted her thoughts. "You only went to high school?"

"I was lucky to make it that far. It was a terrible school, actually. They offered either a totally academic college-prep curriculum or secretarial training. I was painting already, and the only art courses I could take were pastel and charcoal classes once a week with an old woman who encouraged us to draw from nature, but hadn't bothered to look around her for at least thirty years. I used to envy the kids in New York who could go to the artistic high schools."

"But they were extremely hard to get into. Just because a kid was interested in music, like I was, didn't mean he was good enough to get in. Academically, my grades were great, and going to Stuyvesant was what all my teachers recommended. When I look back on it, I realize I was much better suited for a traditional education—even if I'd been accepted by Music and Art or The High School of Performing Arts, it would have been a mistake to go there—but I spent that first year in high school pretty depressed about the rejection."

"What instrument do you play?"

"Piano, of course—isn't that what all up-and-coming parents give their kids lessons in? I was interested in jazz, mostly. I didn't want to play the written notes, I thought I could improvise. But I'd abandoned those pipe dreams by the time I got to college."

"What did you major in?"

"Economics, with a minor in English. I wanted to become a journalist, but I got sidetracked copy-editing textbooks, then business magazines, and here I am." He made himself shut up, lit another cigarette, put his hand across his face to shield the match. "I'm impressed that you continued painting by yourself," he said, anxious to make this a conversation and not a monologue. "You must have had a lot of confidence and commitment."

Confidence? Commitment? Jana felt annoyed. It wasn't as if she'd had choices, she'd simply done what she had to do. She stared at the executive sitting across from her, this man who had wanted to go to Elaine's. All of a sudden she felt the need to justify everything she said. She bit her lower lip, said nothing. It grew later and later while Ed sat there asking mundane questions. What projects did she plan to work on? What were the studios at Yaddo like? Did she know who else would be there?

Jana could have rattled off twenty names—painters, writers, even a composer or two, people she'd met there other summers—but they probably wouldn't have meant anything to Ed, anyway. What he'd really been asking was: did she know what *men* would be there. Yes, there were going to be men at Yaddo too. They might be artists, but they were also men. Natalie had been right: she couldn't run away from men forever.

Ed glanced at his watch: half past twelve. He let his hand cover Jana's. "I wish you'd take a later bus," he said. "I hate the thought of you getting up at seven o'clock tomorrow, missing all your beauty rest." He kept stalling, thinking if it got late enough, if she had another drink, if she could just relax...

"I'll be fine." Jana pulled her hand away and stared down at her wrist. She noticed specks of paint around her cuticles. "Work's more important to me than beauty," she said, forcing a laugh. "I'm anxious to get to Yaddo and settle in." She should have left yesterday. She should have avoided seeing Ed tonight. Besides being bored, she was more than likely screwing things up for The Paperworks Space. "I have to get up early," she said for maybe the tenth time. She moved her chair back, picked up her pocketbook.

Ed smiled, patted her hand again. He insisted upon paying for their drinks and, Jana noted, left a much larger tip than necessary. He walked her slowly back to her apartment, hugged her once again, gave her a quick, amiable peck on the cheek. By this time she was so tired that she made no move to pull away.

ᔆ ᔆ

She must have only been faking tiredness. The moment Ed was gone, she was feeling very much awake. She lay in the single bed, trying without success to focus her attention on the paintings she wanted to work on this summer. ("What do you need a double bed for?" Natalie had asked when she'd moved into this small but affordable apartment, pointing out that a single bed would give her more workspace. And at the time the decision seemed entirely logical). Jana shuddered now to think what might have been going through Ed's mind when he'd seen this bed.

She kept thinking how she'd been anxiously looking forward to seeing him tonight, then how her desire faded as soon as he walked in the door. When she was six months old, she'd gotten very sick. The doctor finally diagnosed it as paratyphoid fever, but she got well before the diagnosis could be confirmed. Her parents must have told that story a hundred times during her childhood. Strange to think of that now, yet that experience seemed typical of her relationships with people: she'll pull all sorts of stunts till she can be sure a person cares about her, then once she's won them over she gets up and walks away from them.

You see, it's not only you, she wanted to reassure Ed. You see, it's not only Ed, she wanted to convince herself.

She turned over; half a turn was all she could manage in this bed, it was as bad as those cots they had at camp. So two people could have slept in it, after all—she and Ed, she and that doctor. But she'd been a child, she'd been ten years old and small for her age; in another five weeks she was to enter sixth grade. She closed her eyes and remembered his warmth against her.

CHAPTER THREE

The Nights Upstate Are Still Pretty Cold

DID SHE really think she could go off to Yaddo and immediately devote herself totally to work, the way she had other summers? Jana slept restlessly. The second night she had a nightmare:

> She was traveling with another woman. They were going to some sort of concert, and started talking with two guys. At first Jana thought her companions were going inside and leaving her behind, but the woman couldn't get tickets. They all went back to the island, intending to get dinner, but one of the guys' fathers appeared, and he kept them talking. It was after midnight and they still hadn't eaten. All the stores on the island were closed—the only thing to do now was to drive back to the coast. Jana said she would drive.
>
> All Jana had on was her nightgown; she wasn't even wearing panties. Her friend cautioned her to get dressed, but Jana laughed at her. Meanwhile, one of the guys cuddled up under her nightgown. She warned him not to do anything, but he wouldn't stop. He kept unrolling his penis, and Jana kept folding it back up again, laughing. At last he got it in her.

*All she could think was that she was driving, there
was going to be blood all over the seat of the car. He
recoiled in horror when he realized she was a virgin.*

She woke from the pain—there was an incredible, burning sensation
in her lower stomach. She lay there, knees drawn up to her chest, rubbing, but it seemed to come from inside her stomach wall. She pressed
one cold hand against her crotch and maneuvered her legs over the side
of the bed. She managed to stand. Now if she could just find the light
switch—she'd forgotten how dark nights were in the country. She
found a lamp on the table, then almost knocked it over trying to turn it
on. She made her way to the closet, wrapped her familiar flannel robe
tightly around her, and rushed down the hall to the bathroom. There
was too much pain to urinate. She gave up and walked slowly back to her
room, groping the wall with one hand to steady herself.

No use going back to sleep now. Jana tossed in the high four-poster
bed with its hooks on the sides that had once held a canopy, a reminder
that Yaddo used to be a private mansion. Damn Ed and his stories about
traveling along the coast of Maine, driving out to the islands. She hoped
now he'd had to sleep on a lumpy mattress.

"It's not sex you're afraid of; it's intimacy, affection." She couldn't get
those words out of her mind. If Natalie had said them, she'd be able to
brush them off as another catty comment. But it was Marilyn's voice she
heard. Jana had called her from Yaddo the afternoon she'd arrived, still
confused about her "evening out" with Ed.

"There's nothing unusual about your reaction," Marilyn began. She
went on to explain that many women became momentarily unrespon-
sive whenever they were with a new man. For some women, she said, the
tension passed quickly. But not everyone was able to become passionate
and emotionally involved even during intercourse; many women kept
themselves at a distance for years, lying there dissociated from their bodies. Frigid, Marilyn termed it.

Now Jana was even more confused. She'd been talking about *sitting*
with Ed, not *sleeping* with him. Besides, she was emotional, constantly
overreacting to little things; she couldn't seem to laugh at herself the way
other people could. The prospect of frigidity seemed not only irrelevant,
but inconceivable.

"What about the way you froze when he took your hand?" Marilyn asked. The phone went silent. Fragments of other conversations could be heard in the background. "The feeling will pass eventually," Marilyn repeated, "but I don't want you to be frightened off by it. That's why I'm telling you this. If Ed understands what you're going through, he might be able to help you. But as it is now, he's probably incredibly confused—one minute you're responsive, then a minute later you withdraw. I think you ought to tell him you like him but that you've always had a problem getting close to men."

"When I first moved to the city I was young enough to get away with saying that. But I'm thirty-four now, for God's sake. If I tell Ed I have a problem getting close to men, it would be like admitting I haven't changed a bit."

"Well, *have* you changed?" Marilyn asked. "It seems to me you're still wrestling with unresolved issues. That's why I wish you'd let Ed try to help you."

"Maybe," Jana said. As always, she wanted to do it all herself, without Ed, without Marilyn. Making a feeble excuse that she needed to unpack, Jana hung up the phone.

She was never going to get back to sleep. The last thing she needed at this moment was to rehash that conversation. She put one pillow over her head, tucked her arm under the other. Already that arm felt numb, as if she'd been lying on top of it all night. She'd go crazy if her whole body felt this way. If she turned out to be frigid, she'd kill herself.

℘ ℘

Jana sat cross-legged on the floor of her studio, looking closely at the milkweed she'd brought back from a walk. It was a depressing stalk, most of the life dried out of it, yet she saw a strange beauty in its form. She pulled apart the pod, letting its hairlike fibers stream through her fingers. She closed her eyes and imagined a man running his fingers through a woman's hair.

She'd been at Yaddo less than two weeks, and already half a dozen similar scenarios had been played out in her mind. She might as well see Ed and get it over with. If necessary, she would force herself to be responsive to Ed's touch, maybe even go to bed with him. Once she'd proved to herself that she wasn't frigid, she could come back and start using her time productively.

The American Association of Women in the Arts was having its monthly chapter meeting next week. She'd only been to five meetings in the six years she'd been a member, but she'd been promising herself she'd get more involved, and it would give her the perfect excuse to return to the city. She called Ed three days before returning. She told him she had a meeting at Columbia Wednesday evening, and he suggested they meet at five o'clock at Teachers, on the corner of 84th Street and Broadway, it was near his apartment and a short distance from Columbia. Also safely public, Jana thought. Her relief was mixed with regret— they wouldn't be alone in a car, or even a gallery.

Once again they sat at an outside table. Broadway at that point went uphill, and Jana found herself tilted uncomfortably as she stared downtown. She stirred the plastic stick in her wine spritzer. A bag lady wearing two sweaters and no shoes crossed the street against the light, dodging traffic. The streets on the west side seemed busier and dirtier than those on Second Avenue, and she felt awkward sitting here, but the radio was blasting inside, and the air conditioning trapped the odor of stale cigarette smoke. "Terry Riley's in residence at Yaddo," she said. "Have you heard his work?"

"Who?" Ed lit his second Camel.

"Terry Riley. He's a minimalist composer, in the Phil Glass/ John Cage tradition. He's done some interesting pieces and gotten quite a bit of attention over the past few years." She'd drawn Terry out about his theories the night before last, hoping to get Ed talking about music and learn more of his interests.

"I haven't been to a concert in months," Ed said. "This summer's been extremely hectic. Frank's family's on Fire Island, and he goes out there Thursday afternoons, which means extra work for Marsha and myself. Today's the first chance I've gotten to enjoy the daylight."

He doesn't seem to be enjoying it very much, Jana observed. Her conversation with Terry had confirmed what she'd already guessed—muscles that tense could never have been adept at playing jazz. Either Ed was trying to put one over on her, or the corporate world had changed him more than he'd realized. "I can get caught up in the pace of the city, too," she said, trying to get an intense conversation started. "But now that I'm away I've been painting street scenes, and the figures are in sharper focus than when I'm seeing them all the time." Jana stretched the truth, this was how her painting progressed other summers.

Ed seemed preoccupied with getting her to the meeting on time. "Just because I'm continually running late doesn't mean I should detain you. Don't pick up my bad habits." It was only twenty to seven when he gulped the rest of his gin and tonic. "Better get you off." He reached for the check he'd asked the waitress to bring with the second round of drinks, then found Jana holding it.

"I invited you this time, remember?"

"Don't be ridiculous; women were born to be treated."

"Not this woman," Jana said. The ambiguity of that statement did not slip by her. She pulled a twenty out of her wallet and left it with the check under the ashtray.

Ed hugged her at the corner, though not even long enough to see if their bodies fit any better than they did that last time. "You don't want to take a walk up to Columbia with me, do you?" she asked. "We could probably both use the air."

"I brought a pile of work home, and I'd better get back to it." He gave her one more brief hug then took a step into the street and stuck his arm out. A Checker cab was right there. She slid in easily despite the portfolio which contained not art but her new nightgown—she'd wanted something lacy on hand tonight, just in case.

She leaned back against the hard seat and recalled the day she'd been in Ed's car—his sheepskin seat covers seemed strangely comforting in retrospect. Two months ago she would have traded anything to be able to relate to Ed as naturally as she did to other people; tonight she was upset because being with him was no different than if she'd met Marilyn for a drink. Dwelling on these thoughts, she managed to thoroughly disorient herself by the time she headed halfheartedly through the courtyard toward Ferris Booth Hall. She certainly wasn't in the mood to see other people: they would be nothing more than reminders of the woman she'd never become. She'd pulled away from Ed once, and it didn't appear he was about to give her another chance. She quickened her pace, jolting at every step, her portfolio swinging at her side, its expensive, lush calfskin brushing against her thin summer slacks.

She was barely in the door when two women accosted her. "We hear you're curating a city-wide environmental art exhibition," they began.

"That's right." Word certainly gets around quickly, Jana thought, bracing herself.

"Sounds like a great idea. Especially for a show sponsored by APL."

"I painted some Central Park scenes a few years ago," the first woman said excitedly. "In several of them I incorporated pieces of rubbish I found lying about. I've got the sketches I did for them at my studio, if you'd care to take a look. I live only a few blocks from The Paperworks Space gallery; you wouldn't have to go far out of your way."

"Thanks for the offer, but I'm afraid we've already selected the participating artists. We had to present their names with the proposal."

"Well, if any drop out, or if you decide to include more people, keep me in mind," she all but pleaded.

"I'll do that." Jana smiled and made her way to a seat that had no empty chairs beside it. She managed to stay awake through a boring speech on feminist issues at cooperative galleries and ran out the minute the meeting was adjourned. She should have realized most of the artists she enjoyed talking to would be summering in Easthampton or Greece. "You can always tell when my painting's not going well," she laughed, stopping herself mid-thought. Usually she was more tolerant of other people. She recalled the first three or four years she'd been in the city and realized that, given the opportunity, she could have been as irritating as what's-her-name.

For the hundredth time Jana wondered why she hadn't arranged to meet Ed afterwards. He'd gone so far as to ask her what time the meeting would be over, but it was right in the midst of his saying how busy the summer had been.

She had no choice but to go home alone and brood. The apartment was a disaster area. It wasn't air-conditioned, and the windows had been locked since she'd left town—opening them now was like opening an oven door. Roaches crawled around the kitchen, even after she had switched on the light. She discovered a box of crackers in the cupboard where they seemed to have been nesting and heaved it out the window into the alley.

"It might be hot here, but the nights upstate are still pretty cold," Jana reminded herself. Angrily she threw two sweaters and five long-sleeve shirts into her mother's old suitcase. As she slammed the lid closed, her eye caught sight of the initials: L.M.S. The M stood for Marcella, the middle name her mother had assumed when she'd gone into the Waves during World War II. Mom's immigrant parents named her Lois, American and ordinary, while she'd yearned for a distinguished, foreign-sounding name. She was exactly the sort of woman who would later name her daughter Jana, the J a guttural Y sound, as it would be pronounced in Dutch. Most people pronounced it instead like a derivative of Jane. Plain Jane. Jane—that was the name of that woman who'd accosted her at the meeting—she'd yet to meet a Jane she liked. But when she was dealing with someone from outside the art community, Jana no longer bothered correcting their pronunciation.

ɛ∕ɔ ɛ∕ɔ

"We've got a meeting with the PR people at APL a week from this Friday, Friday the 13th believe it or not. They requested the artist profiles." Jana had finally settled into a work routine, and Natalie's frantic voice in the telephone receiver was a greater intrusion than usual.

"I finished the profiles before I left," Jana reminded her. "They're in the second drawer down, on the left hand side of my desk. You might want to go over them one more time to make sure we've sidestepped any possibly controversial issues, then get one of the interns to retype them."

"I won't be able to present them with the same authority," Natalie protested. "And it won't look right if the curator isn't at the meeting. Jana, please come down."

"Nat, we've already got half their money, why worry about what impression we're making? I'm in the middle of three large canvases. If I leave now it's going to screw up the flow."

"It's not the only proposal we're ever going to send APL, Jana. I know you went to Yaddo to get some time in front of the canvas, but this meeting's extremely important, and I'm nervous about it. Besides, you'll get a chance to see Ed."

"Who said I wanted to see Ed?"

"You know you do."

"I don't know anything." But Jana gave in and agreed to come down for the meeting.

Thursday afternoon she sat in the nearly deserted gallery, still trying to unwind from the four-hour bus trip, and checked over the profiles.

All these artists had developed interesting theories, but when you looked at the work itself, it was often hard to find the connections. In her introduction, she'd worked to link theory and practice: "Because these eighteen artists have an ecological message to convey, all are concerned primarily with accessibility. Many of them have had extensive training in design; thus their drawings immediately capture the eye. We have carefully selected the sites so that each artist's ecological message will be highlighted by the surrounding environment." She'd gone on for three double-spaced pages—three pages of the same unspecific drivel she'd been writing for years now, long enough to have it down pat.

APL's PR department might expect such hype, but Ed deserved a little more effort. She turned to what she'd written about Lou Daniels' work. Ed had raved to Natalie about how impressed he'd been with Lou's drawings—if she could remember what he'd said, she could astound him with his own insights.

"If she saw me now, Natalie would probably accuse me of using my feminine wiles to impress a man," Jana laughed. And who knows, maybe she was; only she called it "being professional."

℘ ℘

Ed began the meeting by introducing them to Phyllis Mason, vice president in charge of publicity. "She'll be working closely with plans for the exhibition from this point on."

"In addition to media coverage throughout the metropolitan area, we'd like to begin contacting newspapers around the country," Phyllis said as she leafed through the folder Jana handed her. Jana observed her bright blue and green scarf, not tied but carefully threaded through a gold ring—neat but tasteless. Like most PR people, she would probably not be willing to take many chances. "These profiles list the cities where these artists currently live, but they seem somewhat sketchy regarding towns where they grew up or might have studied and taught," Phyllis continued, looking up.

Towns where they grew up, studied, and taught... As Jana opened her own folder to the first artist, she wondered whether Phyllis would want to know about the jails, too. Matt Fillmore had been jailed as a result of his participation in half a dozen anti-war and anti-nuclear demonstrations.

The jail population has probably changed by now anyway, she assured herself, smiling at the thought.

"Let's see," she began, burying her smile in the papers in front of her, anxious to get this meeting over with. "As it says here, he currently lives in Boston, and he studied at Rhode Island School of Design. I know he also spends summers on Cape Cod. As I recall, he's New England through and through, raised in New Hampshire."

Jana was turning to the next bio when Natalie placed a hand on her arm. "Why don't you let us double-check the backgrounds of all the artists, then write them up for you?"

"We were planning to get working on this early next week. Any information you can give us now would be helpful."

Jana and Natalie glanced at each other. Neither wanted to get off on the wrong foot with APL's PR people, but they also worried about giving out inaccurate information and recognized the obligation to their artists not to disclose facts he or she might wish to keep secret.

"Much of the information you need is on file at the gallery. I'll put together as much as I can this afternoon and drop it off tomorrow morning," Jana said before she realized tomorrow was Saturday and the offices would be closed. Then she laughed, and said she'd have it messengered first thing Monday morning.

"Better yet, why not drop it off at my apartment?" Ed suggested. "That way Phyllis will have it early Monday, and we won't lose any time." He'd been preoccupied with work last time he'd seen Jana and wanted to make it up to her.

Jana agreed and jotted down his address, doodling with the letters of his name and reassuring herself this was all in the line of business.

"I notice that seven of these eighteen artists are women," Phyllis continued. "As concerned environmentalists, I assume their interests reach out to feminism as well, and we'd like to interest the feminist press. Can you expound upon these concerns a bit?"

Jana had anticipated this interest. She wasn't involved in the feminist movement herself, but she knew how to go through artistic résumés, selecting feminist credentials for reporters, noting feminist spaces where they'd exhibited, collectives with which they were associated.

"Whew," Jana exhaled as she and Natalie left the building. "Who ever thought a corporate sponsor would become this involved?"

"If this exhibition wasn't also a promotional vehicle, APL wouldn't be investing nearly a hundred thousand dollars," Natalie replied. "Now they've got to make certain their interests are protected." The two women made their way through the 85-degree heat back to The Paperworks Space to go through the files on these artists and make a few quick phone calls to whomever could be reached. "Didn't I predict you'd get a chance to see Ed alone," Nat chortled between calls.

CHAPTER FOUR

This Caring About Others

JANA GLANCED at the clock by her bed: Cinderella's two arms were on top of each other, pointing to the nine. She sat up and dialed Trailways—the morning's final express bus left in twenty minutes; afternoon expresses left at 12:30, 3:00, and 5:30. She pressed the receiver down and called Ed, saying she'd drop by around 11:30. "The earliest bus is at 12:30," she told him.

"What are you doing over the next two hours?"

She had to admit she wasn't doing anything.

"Why not come over now? I'll get coffee started and put on the air conditioner—it'll be nice and cool by the time you get here." He recalled Jana's previous complaints about how hot her apartment was, so he had a feeling that last comment would convince her to come right over.

A half hour later his strong arms enveloped her, pressing her against him despite the heat. "I've got coffee all ready," he said, pulling away. He poured two cups and brought them to the living room, then sat on the sofa, leaving room for her beside him. After a few swallows, he picked up the folder Jana had brought: "Let me take a quick look at these profiles." He still found himself getting mixed signals from Jana; best to keep the business aspects of this visit within reach. Almost absentmindedly he leaned close as he read. Relishing the thought that her body might be able to respond normally after all, Jana moved closer.

The mood was broken by the telephone's harsh ring. Ed reached for it. Jana moved to a chair across the room, but couldn't help overhearing his end of the conversation. "Look, you're extremely lucky this time," he was saying. "You're able to see what's going on." Jana walked over to the large bay window. The last time she'd seen a window like this, complete with a cushioned window bench, had been in her grandmother's house. "We've all been through periods where we need to talk to someone, if only to sort out conflicting feelings. There's nothing to be ashamed of." The window needed washing, but the sun managed to shine through anyway; the apartment was high enough to avoid soot and traffic noise. "It's a beautiful day out," Ed said into the receiver, almost as if reading Jana's thoughts. "Go out on your balcony, read a novel. The work will still be there tomorrow, or the next day. No one's standing over you."

Turning back into the room, Jana held the entire apartment before her. The front door opened onto a long hallway that had two rooms off it: the kitchen and the bedroom; the bathroom, between these, could be entered from either room. The living room itself was huge and had French doors which could be closed to form two rooms. It impressed her as more comfortable than her own apartment, with her paints everywhere and no place to sit except the bed. Two people could easily live here. Taking a deep breath, she recalled an article she'd read a few years ago in *New York Magazine* or *The New Yorker* discussing life in singles bars—it mentioned that people with rent-stabilized apartments were very much in demand. The superficiality had struck her so much at the time that she'd quoted passages to several people. Yet here she was stooping to that level.

"I know, dear, I know," Ed said. "Nobody promised it would be easy. But remember, I'm here. Call me back if you want." He put the phone down, lit a cigarette, and stared off into space, almost unaware of Jana's presence. "I'm sorry," he said finally, expelling a long stream of smoke. "She was desperate, and I didn't want to say I'd call back later."

"No problem. Was that your sister?" Jana was anxious to reassure herself this wasn't some girlfriend.

"No, no. She's an old friend. An old friend with a lot of problems."

"Sounds like she's got a good friend in you."

"She used to, I guess. But there's a limit. I don't want to get caught up in her hysteria again." Ed listlessly stretched his arm across the back of the sofa but got to his feet before Jana could come over to join him. "Why don't we get out of here before Kathe calls back? Come on, I'll treat you to brunch." Jana glanced toward her watch, then decided the time didn't matter, she could always take a later bus. She wanted to learn more about Kathe.

They took the elevator down, walked through the cool marble lobby that was the high point of most pre-war buildings, and emerged onto the hot, muggy street. They walked along West End Avenue in silence among Orthodox families returning from the dozens of synagogues tucked away in this area, the men in heavy black coats that looked out of place in this heat. In stark contrast, there were groups of people with beach towels over their arms.

Ed guided her toward the doorway to Marsala Cafe, a little place on the side street just west of Broadway. "The heat's been getting to me this weekend," Jana said, cautiously eyeing the outside tables. "Would you mind sitting inside?"

"My sentiments exactly. I usually love sunlight, but this humidity is intense even for me." Inside the air-conditioning was on high, but people were packed close enough to absorb any chill. They let themselves be ushered to a booth whose high back gave off a somewhat exaggerated air of privacy.

"Have you ever heard that old saying about how people come to resemble their dogs?" Ed asked once they were seated. "Kathe has long, straight, strawberry blonde hair, parted in the center and curling slightly upward at the ends—just like a Yorkshire terrier."

"And she has a Yorkshire terrier as a pet, right?" Jana replied. She quickly decided on scrambled eggs and let the menu rest unopened on the table in front of her. Her eyes were still adjusting to the darkness after the bright sun outside. Ed exchanged a few words with the waitress; this obviously was a place he frequented.

"Not one dog—Kathe had sixteen when I met her," Ed said, turning his attention back to Jana as soon as the waitress left. "And they weren't pets, they were an obsession."

"You're kidding. How could someone have sixteen dogs?"

"Kathe bred them. She had as many as twenty for awhile there." Ed's voice became animated as he eased into the story: Kathe went with a friend to a dog show, met a guy, and fell passionately in love with him. Kathe, the guy, and all his dogs spent two days together, leaving his RV only for meals. Then he was gone, promising to write and call, but he never did. Kathe started attending dog shows in the area, hoping to run into him. When she finally did, he seemed distant. She reasoned it was because they didn't have enough in common, so she started breeding and showing Yorkies.

"I discovered Kathe with a pack of caged dogs in her living room. Yap, yap, yap all night." Ed yapped himself. "She was thrusting her motherly instincts onto puppy after puppy. I watched her hair grow uncombed while the dogs were treated to Brillcream. A tiny red or blue bow above each ear became two bows, then three."

It was the wrong time to laugh, but the image Ed was presenting of this woman with the uncombed hair was too vivid. Besides, laughing prevented Jana from thinking about how, in teenage rebellion against the suburbia that threatened to engulf her, she'd let her hair go uncombed for days on end. Her mother once spent five hours brushing the knots out. It happened once, and it could happen again, but next time her mother wouldn't be around. If she continued to live by herself, no one would be around to give a damn next time. She might end up an old woman with uncombed hair and sixteen dogs. Or sixteen *stuffed* dogs and one stuffed lion. Even if the dogs were live pets, she doubted she'd care enough to brush their fur and cart them off to shows. She'd more than likely stay cooped up in her apartment with the yapping, paint-stained dogs and a hundred cityscapes.

"Go ahead, laugh," Ed said, interrupting her thoughts. "At least now I can laugh, too. But at the time, I had myself convinced that all Kathe needed was someone who would care about her. And it worked for awhile. She gradually stopped going to dog shows. After a year, she had only two dogs left. You could sit down in her apartment without getting hair all over you. I honestly thought I was helping her."

"It sounds like you *did* help her." Jana reached across the table and gently squeezed Ed's hand.

"I don't know. Sometimes my being with her was more detrimental than anything else. I remember once she arranged to sell a dog to a woman in New Paltz. We drive sixty miles, drop him off, stay and chat with the woman, then drive home. Later that night Kathe became hysterical—the woman mentioned having an ulcer, and Kathe worried it might interfere with the care she would give the animal. The next day we drove back, returned the money, and picked up the dog."

"So having the car made it too easy?"

"Sure. If Kathe'd had to traipse back and forth by train, she might have thought twice about it. And if I hadn't been with her, she probably wouldn't have spent time chatting with the woman to begin with. She'd have never found out about the ulcer, and the dog would be fine." Ed took a long sip of coffee. "I wanted to help, but I couldn't live her life for her."

Jana stared at him. She could easily imagine him chatting away with some woman to whom he was delivering a dog. Ed enjoyed talking, enjoyed learning about people, and easily drew them out. His sensitivity on the phone with Kathe entranced her. But maybe he was fed up with nurturing love-starved little girls who worked out their frustrations through dogs or paintings instead of with other human beings.

"Anyway, enough about Kathe," Ed said, buttering a slice of whole wheat toast. "How's your painting going?" She answered easily. They talked about the panels she was painting, about being out of the city.

"When I first took the job with APL, I thought it would give me more time to spend weekends at the shore, but the longer I'm there, the more I realize I'm happiest spending weekends in the city, working part of the day, maybe taking in a movie or a concert Saturday night," Ed said. "And it's interesting what advantages there are to working under stress: I've been running myself so ragged lately I don't spend much time eating, let alone dreaming about food."

"Aha! The perfect example of the young executive climbing the corporate ladder," Jana teased. "Working so hard you don't even mind that you're working."

"I wouldn't go quite that far," Ed said. "I'm just happy doing what I'm doing."

"You don't sometimes think about moving up in the company? Taking over Frank's job, for instance? Come on, confess. You can trust me."

"I never doubted you for a moment. But seriously, Frank sits behind a desk most of the day. The only people he meets are CEOs and the board of directors. If I had to go to all those fancy luncheons, I'd gain weight again. It might be nice to be making Frank's salary, but I'm not wanting for anything." Ed heard himself talking and did a mental double-take. How many women had he met in the past few years who could tease him about "climbing the corporate ladder"? More to the point, could he have admitted the truth to any of the others? He wasn't interested in those women for the same reason he wasn't interested in Frank's job: they insisted on being part of the social scene, going to all the chic places. Look at Frank running off to the Hamptons every weekend; contrast that with Jana's telling him that growing up in Lakewood had been beach enough for her.

"When I graduated college, I thought I'd become a journalist and write articles that would change the way people look at the world." Ed laughed to think of his younger self and how easily he could share that with Jana; something about her seemed to encourage openness. "After two or three years in the work force, I realized that even political columnists can't bring about such changes. Working as community coordinator for APL lets me at least affect the way a handful of people think."

"It took you two or three years to lose your innocence, did it? You should have been an artist. I moved to New York and spent my first three days here taking a portfolio of drawings around, not making appointments, just footing it from one gallery to the next. I didn't even think to make slides. I lugged around the whole batch, assuming the galleries would be waiting with open arms to receive me. It was a shock to my whole system, not to mention my feet." In a moment of giddiness, Jana let her leg brush lightly against Ed's.

The conversation continued effortlessly until Jana had to go. Ed helped her into a cab, making her promise to call and let him know she'd arrived safely. She climbed aboard the three o'clock bus a split second before it left, and settled next to a thin young man already absorbed in a book. His presence seemed innocuous. After this morning, Ed's was the only body she could imagine getting close to hers.

ల ల

Jana spent Sunday and Monday working on the three-screen panel she'd been describing to Ed over brunch. It juxtaposed three park scenes— Bryant Park filled with winos, a black-and-white imitation of Seurat's *Sunday Along Afternoon the Thames,* and lunch-hour businessmen in City Hall Park. This, along with *Mulberry Street* and a few other paintings, was becoming an unplanned series depicting vanishing neighborhoods. She was filling in the details on the City Hall Park panel when she caught herself copying the ridged gray buttons on the suit Ed had worn to Friday's meeting, three buttons on one sleeve, two on the other. "Good thing I'm not painting the winos," she told herself, though Ed might make an interesting wino. He'd be a little thinner, his face would become drawn, giving him a more serious look. He'd still look damn good. "No he wouldn't," she mumbled, trying to push him from her mind and get back to work. If he were a wino, he'd probably have cigarette holes in that jacket and be wearing a pair of lopsided glasses taped together in ten places, since his contacts would be permanently lost. He'd also be almost totally bald now. "He's not that interesting," she muttered, laughing. But she couldn't convince herself.

She'd talked to Ed Saturday night, and already she was hungering to hear his voice again. She tried to think up some excuse for calling, all the while hating the woman she was turning into. Why couldn't she simply pick up the phone, tell him again she'd enjoyed spending time with him Saturday, say she'd been thinking about him? Because she couldn't. For all she knew, he might have another woman with him; Kathe might be with him, and they might be laughing about her the way they'd laughed about Kathe Saturday morning. She might *hope* that Ed had been thinking about her today, but she had no way of knowing. And she couldn't take the chance of rejection.

The only time she found it easy to reach out to people was when she was functioning as a curator. Then, she could distance her own thoughts and feelings. If a person didn't recall her name, she simply reminded them: name, rank, and serial number. No chance of being hurt. In her curator role, she could call Ed to see if Phyllis had any reactions to the bios she'd given him to bring in. It was safer that way, one professional to another...

Ed started by saying he'd just walked in from a good dinner, "And more than that, a good drink."

"Hard day?"

"Among other things, my air conditioner here is broken."

"I thought you never used it. You said you only put it on for my benefit."

"Well, I want to use it now. Today's been one of the most humid days of the summer."

"It's cool here," Jana said without thinking.

"That doesn't help me any."

"Well, you can come up here. I'll sneak you into my room."

"I want you to come back to the city. We'll have dinner tomorrow night, my treat. This restaurant tonight had one of the best pianists I've heard in a long time. I think you'd enjoy him."

"But you said your air conditioner's broken."

"The air conditioner in my bedroom still works."

The conversation went back and forth for twenty minutes, the two of them laughing, hinting, flirting. By that time, she no longer needed an excuse for calling, but used it anyway.

"I left them with Phyllis' secretary," Ed said, sounding somewhat cool all of the sudden. "If I know Phyllis, she's already begun contacting the various local newspapers, but she seldom has any visible reaction other than to say 'thank you.'"

The minute she hung up the phone, Jana panicked. She'd wanted to feel loose, but not *that* loose. If Ed had been within a hundred miles of her, if there had been the slightest chance he would take her up on it, she'd never have suggested sneaking him into her room. How had the conversation gone off in that direction? There'd been the perfect opportunity to get into a discussion about music when he'd mentioned that pianist, but she'd been too busy thinking about herself to pick up on it. Maybe she ought to quit while she was ahead. She wasn't cut out for this, this, whatever you wanted to call it, this caring about others, this loving.

Tired, disgusted with herself, she settled down on top of the bed. So much for artists being coddled at the colonies, she thought bitterly. A little coddling would help right now, something in the form of a soft down comforter. The blankets here were only slightly better than army blankets, like the ones they used when she went away to camp. She thought about how much she'd hated those scratchy camp blankets—the kids in her bunk had rejected her, she'd felt uncomfortable to begin with, and those blankets had accentuated her discomfort. That's why she'd spent most of that summer in the infirmary. She recalled lying on top of a blanket, watching as the doctor moved slowly toward her. "Doesn't that feel better?" he asked, his lips brushing her newly sprouting hair.

She could feel all the tension in her body. This wasn't camp, it was Yaddo. The people here were friends, they were close associates, they respected each other. Not one person was out there laughing behind her back. There was no reason not to be comfortable here, she told herself, closing her eyes again.

When she was here five years ago, the main source of gossip had been some guy who'd been in residence for six weeks and had brought anywhere from six to ten different women into his room, depending upon who was telling the story. Not very subtle about it either, people said. All the more reason not to tease Ed about sneaking him into her room. She shouldn't have risked it, even in jest. "Kibitzing," as her parents called it, was a throwback to childhood. Since she'd moved to New York, she'd thrust herself into work with a passion that usually didn't allow time for such trivialities.

She crawled under the covers—maybe she could at least dream of Ed. Instead, it was Kathe she dreamt about. Tall, thin Kathe assumed her own small stature. Ed's air conditioner was broken; she kept screaming that her dogs were going to die of heatstroke and it was his fault. She must have had thirty huge, filthy dogs living uncaged in his apartment. At least ten slept in the bed with her. She kept petting them, telling him to brush out their fur so they wouldn't die so fast. Ed tried calming her down by telling her he'd find her a nice apartment with French doors and plenty of light, only Jana knew it was going to be a thousand miles away, far enough that he'd never have to see her. He promised it would be large enough to paint in, but it was a tiny shack with a leaky roof and tar paper walls. "I understand what you're going through," he told her. "But believe me, you'll like it here once you get settled in." And he fondled her hand as he said that.

CHAPTER FIVE

Various Portraits of Women

"YOUR EMOTIONS are strong and sensitive," the fortune cookie prophesied. Jana stared at Marilyn sitting across from her. Marilyn's Indian cotton blouse was cut low—you could see the top of her large breasts over the neck and the outline of her bra beneath the thin fabric. And here I am, prim in my Ship and Shore shirt, as if I'm trying to repress those strong emotions, Jana thought. She ought to take lessons from her outgoing if somewhat disheveled friend. Marilyn looked comfortable and relaxed, no matter what she was wearing; that was one of the things which had attracted Jana to her in the beginning.

Reading the fortune aloud, Jana savored the sweet, broken pieces. "See that," she said. "The baker had foresight to know I'm seeing Ed tomorrow night."

"I thought you came to town because of the DCA commission," Marilyn chided her. The Department of Cultural Affairs was sponsoring an open competition for art in the subways, and Jana was one of the five finalists for the Lex and 86th Street station. If she got the commission, she'd work with a foundry, producing metal cutout figures, sculptures with a painting's one-dimensional surface. Those long underground tunnels would provide the perfect backdrop for her streetwise figures— it was precisely the filthy, changing environment she'd give anything to capture on canvas. The program coordinator called last week, telling her she was a finalist and asking for slides of recent work. As luck would have it, one of the guys she'd gotten friendly with this summer, a photographer, was willing to take the slides for her. The paint wasn't even dry yet when he'd photographed one. She got the slides developed, labeled them, and brought them into town just ahead of the August 27 deadline.

"You know me," Jana said. "Dropping off those slides will be the easy part."

"I used to know you pretty well. Lately, I'm not so sure. I've been trying for weeks to get you to talk about Ed, and you've carefully side-stepped the issue. Now you stand a good chance of getting your work in the subways, and all you talk about is Ed." Marilyn focused her dark brown eyes intently, as if taking a closer look. "Don't forget, this subway commission might come at just the right time to convince Nancy Hoffman to give you a show."

"I wish to hell I could forget," Jana remarked in her obsessive, humorless tone. "It would be much easier if nothing else were riding on the commission." She was coming close to succeeding as an artist: she'd had one-woman shows in major galleries in Philadelphia, Buffalo, Albany, Los Angeles, San Francisco, New Haven; she'd shown in small, out-of-the-way galleries in New York City. Nancy Hoffman had included her in four group shows over the past six years and had several of Jana's paintings in the back room, but sold an average of less than two paintings per year. Reviewing those sales figures, Nancy had told her the work "wasn't quite ready for a show yet." There had been interest in the other paintings, but art buyers, particularly those who could afford Nancy's prices, made their purchases following reviews and other signs that a new artist was becoming a solid investment. Gut feelings counted, reviews tipped the balance. If her work were installed in the subway station, if Jana could get enough publicity . . .

"I'm nervous about that commission, I guess," she continued. "Thinking about Ed helps take my mind off it. It's depressing, though. Suddenly I'm starting to find fault with him again: he's educated, corporate, polished. He wanted to be a jazz pianist as a kid, and I'm unreasonably annoyed that he didn't stick to it."

"That's part of the sexual game," Marilyn laughed. "Haven't you ever seen cats mating? They practically claw each other to death before they finally get together. Humans might be more subtle, but when they're on the verge of something happening, it's typical for people to start putting each other down. You should have heard me when I first met Andy. I was complaining to everyone about how he was a disgustingly macho common laborer. I told myself this was going to be a one-night stand, it could never lead anywhere. Protection, you might call it, covering your losses in case it doesn't work out. I'm certain Andy was doing the same thing with me."

"But I have no way of knowing what Ed's doing or what he thinks of me. I'm not even sure what I think of him. I was probably using the fact that he's a capable executive, a master of the Dentyne smile, as an excuse for flirting with him. That's what upsets me most."

"There's nothing wrong with flirting."

"There is if you have no intention of following through with it."

"But you didn't know that when you started flirting. You don't even know that now."

I wasn't flirting with that doctor at camp, yet look what happened, Jana thought. If she was unable to tell Marilyn about that experience, how could she tell Ed? She used her napkin to wipe the perspiration off her forehead. "I don't know what I'm worrying about," she said finally. "The last time we actually planned to get together we were both too tense to let anything happen. I probably *am* frigid."

"Actually, now that I've thought about it, I'm not convinced you'd be frigid," Marilyn said. "A lot of people who've single-mindedly closed themselves off to men the way you have would probably have frozen when Ed first touched them. It might not mean anything once you two get together."

"It matters now, though. If I don't get past it, there's no way Ed and I will ever, as you put it, 'get together.'"

"Why don't you focus on Ed instead of yourself? Pretend you're talking to a buyer at The Paperworks Space—whenever you talk to people there you're extremely perceptive about anticipating the buyer's reactions. I told you before that if you let Ed in on your hangups it would give him the chance to help you through them, but that's a two-way street— you have to be there supporting him as well."

Jana stared idly around the restaurant. Marilyn was probably right, and that only made her more tense about seeing Ed. Her eyes came to rest on a young woman across the room who shared the table with a four- or five-year-old boy. She wore heavy eyeshadow, matching the blue in her sundress, and a string of fake pearls. Her toenails were painted bright red, glaring out through sandals the same shade of red. Her right hand was folded across her left, so Jana couldn't tell for sure, but she seriously doubted the woman wore a wedding ring.

Jana couldn't take her eyes off this woman whose femininity made her ugly. The past few weeks, certain things about being a woman were starting to appeal to her—she'd even caught herself standing before the mirror playing dress-up. If she gave in to her feminine impulses with Ed tomorrow night, is that what she'd look like? The thought haunted her.

While Jana watched, the woman put on a dark, dull shade of lipstick. She stood up, arranged her skirt, and headed for the door. The little boy had managed to kick his shoes off.

e e

Ed kicked her shoes off, but that was much later. The evening began with a hug no different from other hugs: a simple, friendly greeting Ed might give any woman entering his apartment. Jana pressed her body against him—his chest was strong and firm, bending where she pressed, becoming an extension of herself. After the day's events, she needed all the strength she could muster. The thought of seeing Ed was the only thing that had gotten her through the past four hours.

"How are you doing?" he asked finally, softly.

"Better now," she sighed. She pulled away from him, but not very far away. "I found out that Francis Harriman is one of the DCA jurors. He's going to make sure I don't get that subway commission."

"Why would he do that? Why would anyone . . ."

"I took watercolor and acrylic classes with Harriman at The New School when I first moved to the city. I worked with him for three years and learned an enormous amount—to this day I see the human figure as if through his eyes—but it isn't in me to be a disciple. He wanted students who would follow his methods exactly. He started with watercolor, moved on to oil, and later learned to appreciate the effects of both mediums. He kept hammering at me that I'd never gain complete mastery over my lines, never capture a model's bone structure, until I could work with oil, and at the time I wasn't prepared for that messy involvement with materials." Just talking about it, the image of Harriman's bald head bobbing between the easels in that classroom haunted her. He was a small man but had, as if to compensate, a bellowing voice. When he attacked a student, everyone in the room couldn't help but turn away in embarrassment, and he'd stood beside her, class after class that last term, berating her every stroke. "I dropped the class mid-semester, and he's hated me ever since," Jana continued. "My progression hasn't been under his tutelage, so he's refused to acknowledge it. Even if the other judges like my work, he'll sway them against giving me that commission. I've come so close, and now it's all going to fall through." She leaned against Ed again for reassurance.

"He probably doesn't even remember you." Ed kissed her ear.

"Oh, he remembers me—when I've run into him at parties, he hasn't even given me the time of day."

"You're not easy to forget—you're one of the most capable people I've ever met, and I've met several dynamic businesspeople." Pressing her so closely he could feel her heart beat, he searched within for an experience that would help him identify with Jana's emotional state—all he came up with was not being accepted by Music and Art High School. But no matter how crushing that rejection had seemed, it had forced him to look closely at himself and realize he'd probably never have the spontaneity a jazz musician needed. Stuyvesant made him buckle down and channel his energy; in the end it had been much better preparation for the corporate world.

"We're putting the finishing touches on the exhibition," he told Jana in a conciliatory tone. "A year from now your name will be on display all over the city."

"My name as a *curator*," Jana wanted to scream. Couldn't Ed see that wasn't what she wanted? No, she didn't want Ed to see. She didn't want Associated Power and Light to see her lose her cool. She'd worked hard to be seen as the capable administrator. One evening, a few weak hours, and she could lose it all.

Slowly, walking backward, Ed led her to the huge recliner in the living room. Jana pushed him to move faster. She didn't want to be an administrator, at the moment she didn't even want to be an artist, she only wanted to press against Ed's sturdy, warm body. No, she was not some woman with dyed red hair sitting at a cafe putting on lipstick—she didn't care what she looked like so long as Ed held her. Neither of them gave a second thought to dinner.

"You realize I'm terrified, don't you?" Jana asked in a voice that sounded, even to her, like a ten-year-old's.

"I know that," he whispered. There was a harsh edge to his comment, that same gentle impatience she had detected in his voice the day he was on the phone with Kathe. He's probably telling himself my fears are irrational, Jana realized.

How much did Ed know? In that nightmare she couldn't get out of her mind, the guy in the car recoiled in horror when he realized she was a virgin. The last thing she wanted was for Ed to recoil like that. Marilyn had commented that Ed might be frightened also. If she could get him to admit he was afraid, maybe she could overcome her own fears. "Does sleeping with a virgin frighten you?" she asked, quietly enough that, she hoped, Ed wouldn't hear the word unless he was ready to.

Ed heard. But he'd been waiting since April and could wait a little longer. "I'm not scared," he said, "but I *am* afraid of hurting you." He also said he obviously loved her right now, but he wasn't going to say how he'd feel later because that would only hurt her. He managed, like a high school boy, to work his hands under her blouse. He kicked her shoes off.

"Did anybody ever tell you what a wonderful body you have?" he asked. A wonderful body, yes, but at the moment she was stiffer than those metal cutouts in the subway station would be. He groped for something that would loosen her up. "Too bad you have no mind," he teased, playfully kissing the side of her head.

Jana tensed and drew back. Was this the same man who, not more than fifteen minutes ago, had called her "one of the most capable women I've ever met?" Even in her somewhat frazzled state, she knew he had to be kidding. Relaxing ever so slightly, she broke into a smile. "I can't believe you said that," she mumbled, burying her head in his chest. "I used to think all I had going for me was my mind. A year or two ago I would have killed you for saying that." Tonight she didn't want to be seen as "smart" any more than she wanted to be seen as an artist or a curator. It felt good to be told she had a wonderful body, even if she didn't believe it for a second.

"You've got *everything* going for you," Ed whispered in her ear while she hugged him tighter. She recalled that other night, right before she left town, and how awkward Ed's body felt. But tonight hugging it, winding herself around it, seemed the most natural thing in the world. She never realized her own body could be folded so small.

"Want to spend the night with me?" Ed asked. Jana didn't answer, and Ed interpreted her silence to signify reluctance. "Tonight's probably not the best time for either of us," he continued, not letting go of her.

"It sounds like today wore you out, and you have to get back to Yaddo early tomorrow morning." The exhibition wasn't opening until May, and they'd have to work closely together over the next nine months, regardless of what happened in their personal lives. "I don't want to push you," he continued. "The longer I know you, the more I want our relationship to be more than a one-night stand. But that only works if both people enjoy being together." He'd heard theories that some women don't enjoy sex because they're not introduced properly. Jana deserved better. In the meantime she was willing to fondle him, and he found her touch not only innocent but delightful.

"Comfortable?" he asked.

"Mmm." Last night she'd fantasized Ed asking her to spend the night: she would tell him she was terrified and he would be shocked because she seemed strong and confident; she would ask if he minded if they spent the night cuddling and of course he wouldn't mind and he would hold her in his arms all night and it would be wonderful. But the reality was even better than she'd imagined.

"Promise me you'll spend the night here one of these nights, soon. Even if we just lie next to each other with all our clothes on, I want to spend a full night holding you," Ed said. He'd learned years ago that there was more to making love than fucking. At least for *him* there was.

Promises, hollow promises, Jana thought. That doctor at camp had promised that if she stayed at the infirmary one more night, he'd drive into town and get a pizza better than the one they served in the dining room. And she'd stayed, except for some reason he couldn't leave the camp that night. Tonight's different, she told herself, Ed's different. Ed would be the sort of man who kept his promises.

"Call me," she said when Ed walked her out to get a cab at three AM. He hugged her one final time, but didn't say he'd call.

ᥱ᳚ ᥱ᳚

"Well, look at you. You're a painter now. Your mother always used to tell me how much she wished you'd become a teacher or a social worker; she didn't think you could succeed as a painter. You certainly proved *her* wrong," said a trouble-making aunt who'd cornered Jana after her grandmother's funeral eight years ago.

"My mother never said that," Jana responded.

"Of course she said that, dear. Your mother might not have told you, but she worried all the time."

"My mother always knew I could do or be anything I wanted. She might not have wanted me to become a painter, but she never doubted I could succeed at it." Jana walked away under the pretense of getting more wine.

"Well, I *think* it was your mother said that. Maybe it was someone else," her aunt continued, talking to no one.

The bus must have hit a pothole. Jana woke with a start, her aunt's words making her head swim. She remembered Natalie saying, years ago, in one of those rare moments of insight, that sometimes she felt as if her looks were all she had going for her. "My parents decided early on that I was the pretty one," Nat said. "My sister was the smart one. I think we've both suffered—my sister was twenty-five before she had the courage to wear sexy clothes and jewelry, and look at everything I have to overcome before I buckle down and paint. Parents have no idea what they're doing to kids when they say such things."

Was it possible? Jana's parents had always encouraged her—they tacked her paintings on walls, gave her private art lessons, bragged to their friends about how creative she was. Yet she had no memory of them telling her she was pretty. They commented that she looked nice in one dress another aunt had bought her, a red Scottish plaid with false suspenders and a high collar; Jana could distinctly remember never wanting to wear that dress again. And her mother constantly complained that Jana didn't know how to smile. Or was it that she never smiled? Maybe it was her mother who didn't know how smile and, then, projected her insecurities onto her daughter; she'd done that with cooking, clothes, makeup...

"You have a wonderful body," Ed cooed in her ear. In vain she searched the half-empty bus for a way to discredit his words. She hadn't stood on her head and done tricks last night, she hadn't tried to manipulate Ed into praising her. Here was someone actually telling her how good she was for practically no reason at all, merely for doing what she realized for the first time must have come naturally.

She slid the window open and let herself breathe in the fresh country air. She tried again to remember one time when her parents had told her she was pretty, but all she could hear was her aunt's nauseating Queens accent. All the mirrors were covered that day after Grandma's funeral—there was no way Jana could see herself. Two paintings she had given her parents, amateurish still lifes with extremely flat surfaces, were the only things in that room to distract one's attention.

ↄↄ ↄↄ

Last week some of the Yaddo crowd had gone over to the old mineral springs that once supplied this town's livelihood. They'd invited Jana to join them, but she'd declined—for all she knew, people skinny-dipped. Even if they wore bathing suits or wrapped towels around them, she didn't want her body that exposed.

Last week was before the ache set in. Curled up in Ed's lap, her body had been twisted and turned in completely foreign ways. She got more exercise that night than she usually got lugging canvases around, and ever since, her muscles had been getting back at her, making her pay for all their years of disuse. First her chest and arms ached. Now her neck and shoulders were killing her. Still, she'd probably decline a trip to the springs even if she were invited—what was one night of feeling comfortable with your body, compared to years of keeping it buried under baggy pants and padded jackets?

She sat alone in her room, idly massaging her neck as she stared out the window at a half-moon. The night air helped her concentrate. "I want loving," she used to demand. And her mother would stop whatever she was doing and take Jana in her arms. Jana reached her hand in at the neck of her sweatshirt, found the open collar of her blouse, reached down farther, and clutched her breast. But her hand was smaller than Ed's, too small to contain it all.

She shivered in the cold night air. That dream she'd had the first week at Yaddo flashed through her mind again, only finally she called it by its proper name: a dream and not a nightmare. That pain in her crotch wasn't nearly as strange, or as frightening, as it had been at first. Touching herself right this moment, she could almost, but not quite, duplicate it. As hard as she might try to think of herself as a child, enjoying being cuddled in Ed's arms the way she recalled being cuddled by her mother, there was no denying the fact that she'd become a woman.

She leaned out the window to get a better look at the moon's rays bouncing off the pond and felt her shoulders stiffen again. Love seemed to be having a field day with her body.

No, this wasn't love. "Obviously I love you right now, but I'm not going to say how I'll feel tomorrow or the next day," Ed had said. She wasn't sure what this feeling was, but she had to be careful not to call it "love."

The chilly nights evolved slowly into days that lost the penetrating intensity of their heat, and Jana noticed other changes. Clad in shorts and a man's dyed shirt, she lay in a hammock out near where Yaddo bordered on the harness track, lazily drawing flowers. The hammock rocked every time she drew a line on her sketch pad; her body rocked the way Ed had rocked it in his arms. Over the weekend Ed had driven to Connecticut for his cousin's wedding, and when they'd spoken Monday he'd gone on and on about the flowers he'd seen: violets, brightly colored zinnias, a patch of roses. "I've been in the city so long I'd forgotten what it was like to see flowers cultivated on lawns," he said. "They seemed the image of health." She thought about how often this past week she'd walked the grounds, picking daisies and pulling off their petals: he loves me, he loves me not. Or on alternate days: I love him, I love him not. But no, she couldn't tell Ed that quite yet.

Jana sketched herself as a healthy flower. It was only a matter of time now. There was an urge in her body that cuddling could no longer satisfy. They would take it slow. For the first few nights, she would ask Ed to take precautions. She was sure now that he cared enough for her that he wouldn't object. The free-sex craze had passed—people worried about AIDS and herpes—asking a man to take precautions was no longer an unusual request, Marilyn had explained. After she lost her virginity, Jana would make an appointment with a gynecologist. Maybe she would get pills, maybe a diaphragm; she didn't have to decide at the moment.

Various portraits of women played themselves in her mind, but her thoughts came to rest on the famous surrealist photograph of Duchamp as Rrose Selavey. How easy it had been for him to dress in drag and take on the woman's identity. The finished image was nothing but a trick, a mental game which lent itself to photography. The distancing of that final print would be more difficult for a woman to attain, Jana realized now. Regardless what Marilyn said about frigidity, Jana knew no woman would want to be that out of touch with her emotions. She could no longer paint as she'd been painting for years—holding herself back, not letting her vision stray from the external object. She wanted to paint the portrait of herself as a woman, not a woman in some flower mask.

She made a dash for her studio, grabbed a stubby piece of charcoal, and drew her eyes, a little below the horizon line: thick, black, almost closed. Then the heavyset face (much heavier than the mirror revealed her, as if she were trying to let Ed's heavier body share the picture). But no, there was something else about that heaviness, something significant she couldn't pinpoint. She stared ahead, blankly. Ed's words echoed through her mind—the number of calories in a potato chip, not having time to dream about food. Had he been trying to tell her he'd been fat not long ago?

Jana recalled Matisse's "Odalisque" series—the fat women reclining on couches, sensual, beautiful, and the women Titian painted, and Rubens. Fat men could be beautiful also. Any man was beautiful if you cared enough about him. The challenge was to make *herself* attractive.

She drew her lips, thick and pressed firmly together, resolute. She drew a cap for the skull, reminiscent of the bathing caps she'd worn as a child. Responding to the pressure of that cap, she drew wrinkles on her forehead. She ran two dark lines along her left cheek, where she'd smudged charcoal a few minutes ago. She outlined the faint moustache that had grown back again, its shadow on the lip and chin. Finally, a little slower now, she placed the entire face in shadow.

She stepped back to look—something was missing. "You have a wonderful body," Ed had told her. Not until now did she recall the other half of his comment: "Too bad you have no mind."

"It's like you're making love with your mind," Harriman had quipped thirteen years ago, in one of the last classes she'd taken with him. She'd been going through a crisis with perspective, every figure she drew seemed foreshortened. Gary Jeffreys, her closest friend in that class, had set up his easel next to her—she'd been guiding her arm to give her a sense of the follow-through. After Harriman's comment, she looked down and saw the bulge in Gary's jeans. If she hadn't been absorbed by the painting she would have checked her responses before Gary got to that point, yet it was precisely that closeness, that sharing of the mind in the body, that had been important to her ever since. She'd used that memory to console herself every time she saw Natalie or Marilyn rushing about in their endless affairs.

Now all of the sudden she found herself needing something more from Ed, and her mind was holding her back. She envisioned the brain lines shown in anatomy books, and drew them across the forehead, holding her breath with each stroke. The smudges on her cheek now seemed an extension of those heavy lines. Yes, that was how she felt: weighed down by mind, cowering, clenching her eyes against the weight. But things didn't have to stay that way. With white paint she went over those horrifying brain lines, trying to blend them in, soften their effect. She ran her fingers roughly across to smudge them further, wiped the paint off on her shirt, then put her hand to her forehead as if trying to relieve a migraine, to free herself from that weight she'd clung to all these years. She had left no room for heart. The mind had covered over her body even, the body Ed had said was beautiful, the body she was suddenly, unexpectedly, proud of.

At last she let her eyes open. The pictured self greeted her boldly, un-ashamed. It was almost, but not quite, feminine—almost, but not quite, human. She reached for the can of unscented hairspray and sprayed the canvas. Hairspray was cheaper than the sealants sold in art stores—everyone she knew used it—but she'd fought against that reminder of femininity until this summer. Lost in thought, she sprayed much heavier than necessary. Yesterday a wasp had gotten into her studio and she'd sprayed it in precisely this manner. She'd watched the residue weigh down its wings, watched it struggle to fly, buzzing angrily, until it finally lay on its back, its legs kicking, dying slowly. She hadn't thought twice about killing it.

CHAPTER SIX

Self-Portraits

THERE WERE more self-portraits over the next ten days—strange, abstract works: the top of a head as if in a rear-view mirror, the side of a face reflected in a chrome doorknob—fragments of herself she was willing to accept now. Jana painted frantically, working directly on the canvas, without sketching, without much forethought whatever. The realization that she'd soon return to her normal routine, giving up these hours upon hours with nothing to do but paint, didn't bother her. The work she was beginning now would hopefully carry over. She'd be able to spend all day reviewing drawings at The Paperworks Space or working on the forthcoming exhibition, then come home and concentrate fully on her own work. And maybe, just maybe, after a few hours of painting, she'd get together with Ed. New York City suddenly seemed packed with all the excitement she'd experienced when she'd moved there as a twenty-year-old.

She decided to go back a day early. "I have to meet with APL's PR department Monday afternoon," she told the Yaddo administrators, keeping a delicate edge of regret in her voice. "I need Sunday to unpack and reorient myself." A professional appearance, as guest curator as well as painter, couldn't help but work to her advantage next time she applied for a residency. If the truth be told, she was going back on Saturday because of Ed. He'd be meeting her at Port Authority, "to help you home with your luggage," as he put it. There was a good chance they'd have one night together before resuming their professional interaction, but she was determined not to set her hopes on that happenstance.

Ed watched her step down from the bus, carrying her portfolio. She noticed his expression change to amazement as the porters handed her three suitcases and five canvases tied together, facing inward to protect their surfaces, which had been stowed in the luggage compartment. Lifting the suitcases immediately set him off balance. "What do you have in this one, rocks?" he asked.

"Painting supplies," Jana laughed. "What did you expect?"

He hadn't known what to expect this time. "You should have told me you had this much gear. I'd have driven up to Saratoga and gotten you."

"I guess I'm just used to managing by myself." Jana laughed, hearing the echo of her comment from the time when Ed had offered to drive her back to the gallery. "Let's not have a replay of *that* day," she silently admonished herself.

They'd barely set everything down in the corner of Jana's studio when someone knocked on the door. Jana opened it to admit a young guy with blonde hair longer than Jana's and Ed's put together, tied back in a ponytail. "I thought I heard someone in here," he said as he barged in.

"You heard right. Niels, meet Ed. Ed was kind enough to help me schlep everything home."

"I just thought I'd bring your mail down," Niels said after exchanging a few words with Ed. "There's also a slip for a package at the post office—they refused to leave it with me."

"I'll get it Monday, thanks. Want to sit down? I think there's some cold beer in the fridge."

"I'm afraid I can't stay, I've got to get to work." With a quick nice-to-meet-you in Ed's direction, Niels took off.

"He's an actor," Jana told Ed when Niels left. "Works as a waiter between jobs. He's on the road a lot too, and we've worked out an arrangement to take in mail and look out for each other's apartments." She leafed quickly through the mail, opening four or five pieces and putting them in a separate pile on the table.

Niels' intrusion reminded Ed that Jana probably had a million things she wanted to get done today. But he'd promised himself he'd invite her back to his place, and he had wine, bought the day before, chilling in his icebox. He had to at least give it a try.

"Sounds good," Jana said, getting up and pulling a few things together. "But why don't we walk at least partway over? Even short legs get cramped from sitting in the bus."

"Fine with me," he lied. The last thing he expected was that she'd agree so readily. He'd settled in to work this morning and had gotten more involved than he'd planned. He hadn't even had time to change the sheets on his bed.

Jana grabbed a sweater out of her suitcase. "Should I bring a night-gown?" she asked, almost as an afterthought, as they were leaving her apartment.

"That might not be a bad idea. You'll probably feel a little more secure if you're wearing something."

She bit her lower lip. "Ed's only looking out for me," she tried to tell herself. "He has no way of knowing I sat by the window imagining him cuddling my naked body."

They sauntered over to the park and headed for the reservoir. Run-ners of all shapes and sizes approached and passed, along with walkers going in both directions. Most of the runners were unencumbered, wearing shorts or cut-offs and tee shirts, one or two with money belts on, many with earphones, one guy with a backpack. One runner dropped change out of her pocket, stopped to pick it up. A squirrel paced Jana and Ed's walk for a moment, almost hidden in the tall grass sloping downhill beside the path. A little lower, a few bikes went by.

"The park seems so much quieter on weekends, when the drives are closed," Jana said.

"It seems natural to me. I guess I only get here on weekends."

"When I'm trying to sketch, I come here in the middle of the week. There are fewer people, it's easier to focus on one person or group with-out interruption."

They sat down on the benches facing the south gate. Two horses passed on the bridle path, below them. A few runners leaned on the buil-ding or benches and did stretching exercises. Others stopped for drinks at the fountains, splashed water over their arms. "Want a drink?" Ed asked.

"Not here, thanks."

So they headed on. There were a dozen ballfields on the Great Lawn, with softball games going at right angles to each other. On a corner of grass beside the field, what looked like forty ten-year-olds in Cub Scout uniforms were goofing off as they did warm-up exercises, led by three men. Some of the boys were wearing their baseball gloves already. When the exercises ended, there was no open field, so they played in the same stretch of grass. "Where's first base?" one boy screamed. And another: "That's not where the catcher is." Jana and Ed laughed at the interchange. Finally one of the men said he'd set up the bases.

They wandered toward the children's playground. Ed started for the benches to the left of the thick gates, but Jana sat on a swing, so he eased himself onto the canvas swing beside her. "This is the one place I never have to worry about sitting alone." Jana let the ropes sway gently as she talked.

"Worry no longer," Ed swayed closer.

"It never ceases to amaze me how children have to be *taught* how to play sometimes. That's something I was totally oblivious to when I was growing up. I never played well with other kids, but nobody ever taught me how, either. I was ten or twelve before I learned how to pump my legs on a swing. Someone always had to push me."

Before Jana realized what was happening, Ed was standing behind her. "Do you want to go fast or slow?" he asked, giving a gentle push.

"Fast." Jana took firm hold of the ropes. "No, slow! Slow!" she shouted a moment later, laughing as Ed pushed with all his might, and she went zooming so high she could feel the bars holding the swing shake.

"Say please," Ed called, pushing as hard as ever. "Say pretty please with hamburger on it." And then, a moment later: "Say it like you mean it." At last Ed gave in, the swing slowed, Ed walked to the front and Jana leapt into his arms.

Jana saw there was no one in the sandbox. She wandered over, picked up a twig, and began drawing. She drew Ed's face, half-portrait, half-caricature, then quickly rubbed it out. "I can't draw well when someone's looking over my shoulder," she laughed, tossing the stick away.

"You artists are never satisfied," Ed teased. "I thought you caught my resemblance perfectly."

"If you're nice, maybe I'll draw you for real sometime," she said, heading out the gate again. "When my parents used to take me to the beach, I remember drawing in the sand. They'd try to get me into the water or to hunt for sand crabs, but I'd just pick up a popsicle stick and start drawing."

"Your parents must have loved that," Ed teased.

"They wondered what was wrong with me," Jana answered seriously. They walked along in silence once again. It was one of those in-between days when the walkers and the people sitting in the park were dressed for anything. Some wore long-sleeve shirts, a few men wore ties and jackets, one girl passed wearing a leather jacket. Many people carried sweaters or sweatshirts, some tied them around their waists.

"I'm struck by the difference between those people who come to sit in the park, and those passing through on their way somewhere," Jana commented as they sprawled on the grass near one of the entrances.

"I never noticed it before."

"It's easier to see in the women. Take that woman in the long dress and shawl, carrying a MOMA bag. You can tell she's doing other things today."

They began guessing at the relationship between people who passed them. "Friends," Ed said, pointing to two women seated across from them. "Probably close friends, they've been friends for ten years, at least. Since high school."

"No, I'd say they're sisters. The hair color's different, but look at the shape of their faces. Look at their mannerisms."

"You think you know it all, don't you?" Ed joked.

"I just know what to look for. Chalk it up to an artist's eye." A very pregnant woman walked beside a young man in slacks, sports coat, tie, and sneakers. Neither looked overly happy. They walked together but didn't touch. Jana and Ed both watched, but seeing them dampened the game a bit.

Then, noticing how many people were carrying maps and cameras, they played at guessing where they were from. "How about that guy with the two cameras?" Jana asked.

"Definitely cosmopolitan but dressed too warmly. Montreal." Ed guessed.

"Nope. I'd say he's from New York City, probably the Upper West Side."

"What makes you think that?"

"He's carrying two cameras, not one, which indicates a photographer more than a tourist."

"So he's a photographer from Montreal."

"Nope. He's walking straight, he's looking around him just to check things out, not with any real interest. Which means he's headed somewhere and knows where he's going."

"I never found strangers so interesting before," Ed commented, half to himself. He got up to stretch, but Jana took it as a sign to leave. "This way," he said, grabbing her arm.

"No, it's this way."

"Go see." They walked to the avenue a few hundred feet away. Sure enough, Ed was right, Jana would have walked toward Fifth Avenue.

"Sorry. I guess I got turned around."

"I'm delighted; it proves you don't know everything, after all."

"I was preoccupied."

"With what, I wonder?" Ed mused. Jana didn't bother answering.

Ed recalled the last time they were together, when they'd gotten tangled up in each other and didn't bother with dinner. "How about we stop for a bite on the way home?" he suggested.

"That sounds fine, except I don't want any arguments this time: you helped me get the stuff home from the bus station, the least I can do is buy you dinner."

Ed hesitated. "I was thinking of someplace special, maybe Tavern on the Green as long as we're in the park . . ."

Jana wasn't sure whether to laugh or cry. This difference in their lifestyles added to the tension she felt with Ed: his apartment with bay windows looking out on West End Avenue compared to her shabby studio overlooking an air shaft, his car, his well-polished shoes compared to her paint-stained sneakers. "Ed, look," she began, "I know you make a good salary, but I have a job, too, and I'm not paid that poorly. I might choose to spend most of my earnings on painting supplies, but that's my choice. So if I want to buy you dinner tonight, or any other night, that's my choice, too."

"I wasn't implying . . ."

"I know you weren't implying, but I *was*. Besides, letting you pay for things makes me feel obligated to you, and I don't think you want that any more than I do. It'll be easier if we split things, at least for now."

Splitting was preferable to her paying for dinner tonight, Ed consoled himself. But instead of "someplace special" he led her toward a moderately priced but comfortable nouveau French place. It was also quicker; the longer they sat there, the more anxious he was to take Jana home with him.

He led her into the apartment, poured a glass of wine. "Wine! I might have guessed it," Jana exclaimed. She told him about painting the park panel, and how she'd considered depicting him as a wino.

"So, how'd I look?" Ed asked.

"Great, as always. But I'm prejudiced."

On that note, Ed left her alone in the living room. Jana sat on the Danish Modern couch, noticing how different the room seemed when Ed wasn't around. The painting above the couch, imitation Jackson Pollock at his worst, appeared chosen by a yuppie decorator to echo the various shades of blue used as accents around the room. She crossed her legs, took a sip of wine. It was red wine and should have been room temperature—chilling it had made it lose what little flavor it had. Here I go again, putting Ed down to protect myself, she thought, recalling Marilyn's comment. People were *worse* than cats; they tried to suppress the tension. She took another sip of wine. If she wasn't careful it was going to give her a headache. Red wine always did.

She picked up a throw pillow and hugged it against her chest, running her fingers through the fringe. She wondered if she'd ever let Leroy out of the closet. "Just think, a real lion, I have a real lion now," she whispered to the pillow. She envisioned walking into the bedroom and discovering that Ed, too, slept on Miss Piggy sheets.

༄ ༄

In fact, the sheets were a solid color, mint green, and the pillows had plain white cases. It must have been well after midnight when they climbed into bed. They cuddled for a while. Carefully, Ed began fondling her clitoris. "Look at how wet you are," he said.

"I'm sorry." Embarrassed, Jana drew away.

"It's okay," Ed whispered. "You're wet because you're stimulated. That's what I hoped would happen." He pressed her against him.

Certainly Jana expected more to happen tonight, but she had to admit she was relieved. She was still on a country schedule of turning in early and getting up at the crack of dawn. She shifted away from him as her eyes grew too heavy to stay open. He began snoring lightly a moment later.

Suddenly she found it impossible to relax. The right side of her body wasn't used to being pressed against a mattress. She turned over; Ed's warm flesh blocked her intake of air.

In the middle of the night, waking to find her staring off into space, Ed suggested they change sides. His careful, hairy legs slid over her. Jana drifted off to sleep so quickly one might have thought she was in her own bed.

"That's your good side, isn't it?" Ed said the next morning. "Why didn't you say something last night?"

"I didn't want to disturb you."

"So you lay there like a dodo," he teased. "We'll mark that side of the bed with an x. It will be yours from now on." He had as much as said that he wanted her back! It might not be now, but it wouldn't be never after all. Jana was so disconcerted that she poured orange juice, thinking it was milk, straight from the carton into the coffee Ed had set on the kitchen table.

"I'd best get home and start unpacking," she said soon after breakfast. She hadn't fantasized about the "morning after" part and wasn't certain what a woman was supposed to do at this point. Much as she wanted to spend the day with Ed, she assumed the suggestion should come from him. "Will I see you at the meeting tomorrow?" she asked on her way out.

"You'll see me at the meeting," he said, kissing her forehead. "If not before that," he wanted to add, but she seemed anxious to get home. "The meeting tomorrow afternoon," he repeated behind the closed door.

ᨠ ᨠ

Jana retrieved the suitcase from the corner of her room and began putting clothes back in her closet, pretending she was hanging slacks up in Ed's closet. She folded sweaters into the drawers of the old maple dresser she'd found on the street two years ago, imagining herself placing them in a drawer Ed had cleared out for her. She called Marilyn, intending to give her a full report, but realized there were aspects she preferred to keep to herself.

First thing Monday morning, she stopped at the post office. The package turned out to be her slides, returned from DCA with a xeroxed letter: *We regret to inform you that you were not among the final artists selected to receive an Art In Public Spaces commission. Please bear in mind that only two commissions were awarded, and this rejection does not reflect upon the quality of the work reviewed. We hope you will apply for future commissions sponsored by the Department of Cultural Affairs, which will be announced in the near future.* "I knew it," Jana told herself, "Harriman succeeded in blocking me."

The time with Ed set her off balance, the rejection letter knocked her down, and her poise was stretched to its limit by Monday afternoon's meeting. A glance at the first three items on the budget Phyllis had outlined for the gala didn't help:

$47,500 for catering (the original budget listed $2,000)

$3,000 for speaker fees ($1,000 on Natalie's budget)

$3,500 for the band (a new expense)

When parking, limos for dignitaries, flowers, and other miscellaneous expenses were included, funds appropriated for the gala alone totaled $62,400. Jana and Natalie had expected the entire exhibition to cost less than $69,000. Jana jotted a few calculations on her notepad: eighteen artists, with six pieces each, totaled one hundred and eight pieces. The average drawing sold for $900. If, instead of staging a lavish reception, APL were to purchase half the pieces in the exhibition, they would still have almost $14,000 left in the budget for a gala reception. Even The Paperworks Space board of directors would laugh in her face if she suggested such purchases, she realized, smiling shyly in Ed's direction. Ed's return glance seemed to whisper "later."

Phyllis explained that Windows on the World didn't have room for a dance floor, but the Vista Hotel, on the second floor of Tower Two, had a lovely ballroom, and their food was excellent. "If we can put on a grand enough gala *and* can get a guarantee of coverage from the all the local TV channels and at least two major networks, I'm certain Ed Koch can be persuaded to give the keynote address," she concluded.

"I agree it's a good idea to aim for weighty political speakers, but we also don't want to forget this is an artistic event," Natalie commented. "How about trying to get Kitty Carlyle Hart to speak as well? As executive director of the New York State Council on the Arts, she might offer a nice balance to political concerns."

"I'll check into that," Phyllis promised, jotting down the name but obviously not willing to commit herself. "Any entertainers you think might be appropriate? What we're looking for is someone with a big name, but not the same people who are continually doing benefits."

"You mentioned hiring a band," Jana said. "Perhaps we could begin searching for musicians who draw crowds?"

"Skitch Henderson, perhaps?"

Jana chuckled. "I was thinking more of Miles Davis. Someone with a reputation for ground-breaking work in his art form, someone who will compliment the artists we're presenting."

"Well, we don't have to decide today," Phyllis said, realizing this aspect of the meeting was headed nowhere. "The gala's not until just before Memorial Day. I think if we have a list of people to speak with by November, we'll be fine. That way we can begin final arrangements before the holidays."

Jana felt as if she'd been given a stay of execution. But as always, Natalie broke the spell. "Miles Davis only works high-paying jobs and third world benefits," Nat commented as they headed back to the gallery. "Besides, he doesn't play dance music."

"Then we're back to Skitch Henderson," Jana quipped. "I wanted to get them thinking in terms of a jazz sound. Ed might come up with some ideas, too."

"I should have known you were thinking of Ed."

"Phyllis didn't bring up Matt Fillmore," Jana said, changing the subject. "I can't believe she hasn't read between the lines of his bio yet."

"Don't kid yourself," Natalie cautioned. Certainly everyone at APL knew Matt's reputation by this time, but they wouldn't broach the subject unless someone from The Paperworks Space did. Everyone, including Natalie, was still hoping there would be nothing to discuss.

At least one good thing had happened today—Jana was meeting Ed for dinner. She took the slides returned from DCA out of her desk drawer, opened the padded envelope, and held them up to the light. They'd been carefully inserted back in their plastic cases. If she didn't know better, she'd think no one had looked at them. "It doesn't matter," she told herself. "My work's evolved so much in the past month that these paintings feel ancient now."

☙ ☙

She spent Monday night with Ed, then they planned to meet at his apartment again Wednesday night. Jana heard the music coming from behind Ed's door as she walked down the hallway. "I want you to hear this," Ed said almost before he'd kissed her. She saw the album spinning on the turntable and picked up the jacket lying on the sofa—*Sonny Rollins: Way Out West.*

"I came home tonight and dug it out of the back of my closet. It's got to be ten years since I played it," Ed told her. "This was my favorite album as a kid. Listen."

Jana *tried* to listen, but she was too tense. She'd always been told she had a tin ear. Would Ed lose interest in her if she couldn't share music with him?

"This album came out in 1957, just after Rollins split from the Max Roach Quartet. Not many people knew about Rollins in those days," Ed told her proudly. "I was fourteen—it was the last year I took piano lessons. My teacher saw these arrangements as an inspired way to entice kids who'd rather have guns hanging on their hips than be sitting at some dumb piano." He sat down beside her on the sofa. Jana closed her eyes and leaned her head on his shoulder, hoping if their bodies were close enough he wouldn't notice her lack of appreciation. "I'd sit in my room with the door closed, playing this over and over on my old monaural record player. Then, beginning with my junior year I got tied up applying to colleges, then the pressures of school. . ."

Suddenly a broad smile crossed her face. "Is that 'I'm An Old Cowhand?'" she asked in amazement.

"Yep," Ed said. "These songs were inspired by Rollins' first trip to the West Coast. Aren't they great?"

Jana sat up straight and shifted to face him. "It's amazing," she began. "I can hear the music! I can even recognize the tune!" She was beaming so proudly that Ed had to laugh at her. "You don't understand—I've never been able to hear music before. It usually runs together in my head and sounds more like noise than a melody. But I can hear it. I can actually hear what Rollins is doing!"

This time Ed let loose with a loud laugh. But quickly he joined in her excitement. "The best way to understand jazz is through the really simple melodies, where the musicians keep coming back to the same place. Wait—I'll show you." He searched through the box of records he'd dragged from the closet and found John Coltrane's "My Favorite Things." He cleaned the record off with his Diskwasher kit, then held it up to the light to check for scratches before he put it on the turntable.

Jana listened and listened. "I'm not hopeless, after all!"

"Far from it. As a matter of fact, you give *me* hope," Ed said, drawing her close again. Her innocence brought back his own naïveté, yet she was also quick to catch on. "It's been a long time since I've just sat back and listened to music—I mean just listening, not judging, not seeing it as an event APL might be interested in funding, not monitoring a concert series already receiving support."

"What made you bring out these records tonight?" Jana asked.

Now it was Ed's turn to smile broadly. "I've been planning to listen to Rollins since that day over the summer when we had breakfast. Hearing you talking about your painting brought back all the memories."

"Has it really been that long since you listened to music?"

"The first few years I was working in the city, friends and I used to go to concerts every so often. Then I started seeing Kathe all the time. My friends didn't especially like her, and I guess I let too many friendships drop. The music sort of dropped along with them."

A blank look crossed Jana's face. Ed asked what was wrong. "I was just picturing you getting involved with me now," she began, "or hoping you'd get involved with me now."

"I'm hoping the same thing."

"What about those old friendships?"

"Are you kidding?" Ed laughed. "Those friends will love you."

೦೨ ೦೨

"I wonder how long I'll be able to hold onto Ed if we do nothing more than sleep beside each other," Jana was thinking when she walked into her apartment on Thursday morning. He kept insisting there was no rush, but still...

There was a message on her machine to call Steve Whitman at the Walker Art Center in Minneapolis. "Back to business as usual, even for virgins," she thought dryly. "Whitman probably wants to know if Walker can get the environment exhibition after it closes here." She hated it when people called her at home about gallery business. She'd wait and return the call from work.

"The reason I called," Steve Whitman began while Jana pressed the receiver to her chest and looked over a letter the intern had typed, "is that Sara George, one of our former administrators, now works for the Department of Cultural Affairs in New York City. She saw the slides you submitted for a possible commission over the summer, and suggested I get in touch with you. We're in the process of curating an exhibition scheduled for this coming March entitled 'Three Artists, Three Cities,' and Sara thought I should I consider your work. I realize it's short notice, but could you rush copies of the slides to me?"

Jana caught her breath. "I have them right in front of me," she said. "If you give me the address, I'll get them to the post office before six tonight." She scribbled the address down, got off the phone, typed a new label, placed it over the DCA address, and told Natalie she had to run. "You won't believe what Whitman wanted," she added, hurrying out the door. Harriman might have prevented the DCA commission, but he had no control over other invitations resulting from her efforts.

"Sara George." As she headed for the post office, Jana repeated the name Steve Whitman mentioned. She couldn't recall having heard it before, but she owed Sara George one hell of a favor now. Much as she would have liked to suppose her paintings had been noticed on their own merit, she'd been around the scene long enough to realize her résumé, with "Curator: The Paperworks Space" boldly on the top, had made the first impression.

Before the month was out, Steve Whitman had called to say he found her work perfect for the Three Artists, Three Cities show; his secretary would be mailing the contract next week. Before the month was out, Jana found herself spending every night at Ed's apartment. They seemed to grow closer every night—emotionally, if not physically. "This *is* making love," Ed assured her.

CHAPTER SEVEN

The Comfort She'd Wanted

ED WALKED into the restaurant with that same peacock strut Jana had observed last March. He kissed her hello, sat down, and ordered a split of champagne. "Here's to Frank's levelheadedness," he said, lifting his glass. "I told him we're seeing each other."

"What? Why?" Jana's first swallow went down the wrong pipe. She'd heard stories about men spreading their romantic conquests throughout the office, but she hadn't expected it from Ed.

"Hey, take it easy," Ed said. "I *had* to talk to Frank. It's one thing to have a few dinners with someone who works for an organization we're funding. Even spending a night or two with them isn't exactly condoned by the higher-ups, but everyone tends to look the other way. Seeing that person on a regular basis is another story, and we've been together a month now."

Trying to stay calm, Jana asked what Frank had said. Ed's chest puffed out again. "He told me what I did on my own time was my business. He assumed I was a consenting adult when he hired me, and he'll continue to expect adult behavior from me. Then he went on to praise the work I've done so far on the exhibition."

"That's all?"

"Just about all. There were the usual formalities—he assured himself that my interest in you had no bearing on my recommendation of The Paperworks Space for funding, and he warned me to let him know if I saw our relationship starting to interfere with my job. All said and done, it wasn't nearly as tricky as I'd feared."

Jana set her glass down firmly on the table. "What if he'd said no?" Ed was letting Frank call the shots. If Frank had said they couldn't see each other, he'd have sent her back to her own apartment. It was that scene at camp all over again. "You have to go back to your bunk tomorrow," the doctor had told her. "The counselors are getting suspicious because you're here all the time."

"Hey, Frank didn't say no." Ed's voice was saying. "At worst, I imagined he might take me off the exhibition, but he wasn't going to insist we stop seeing each other. Basically, I think he's happy for us. His last words were 'enjoy yourself.'"

The same thought simultaneously crossed both their minds: *Little does he know.* They burst out laughing. "Does Frank suspect there's a scared high school virgin underneath this polished surface?" Jana asked when she'd caught her breath again.

"There won't be for long," Ed promised.

೧ ೧

Everything seemed simple while Jana was at Yaddo: she'd lose her virginity within a week at most, then she'd see a gynecologist. But she'd been with Ed for over a month now, and she was still a virgin. The longer she put off going to a doctor, the more intimidating the prospect loomed. No matter how responsive she might be to Ed's gentle fingers, she didn't trust the excitement to continue. Some manipulative doctor could touch her in the wrong place, at the wrong time, and that would be the end of it. All she needed now was to wind up with another Dr. Anderson.

She'd gone to Natalie's gynecologist six years ago. Before even starting the examination, Dr. Anderson asked if her periods had been regular, then scolded her viciously when Jana responded that she didn't know. After what seemed a grueling examination, she diagnosed a yeast infection and gave Jana a tube of medication, along with an applicator that looked like a gaping needle, instructing her to apply it twice daily. "Isn't there a pill I can take instead?" she pleaded, revolted at the prospect of touching herself "there." Making no effort to hide her disgust, Dr. Anderson asked if she had ever thought of seeing a psychiatrist. An hour later Natalie assured her crying friend that yeast infections eventually went away on their own. Wrapping the tube and applicator securely in a brown paper bag, Jana threw it in a garbage can.

Thinking back on it now, Jana felt a chill that probably had more to do with this paper gown that was supposedly covering her. It didn't wrap all the way around and had ripped when she'd lifted herself onto the high table. Recalling Ed's promise that there would be more, and better, lovemaking to come, Jana waited nervously for this new doctor. The stirrups, threatening a few inches away from her unshaven legs, didn't seem as far apart as they had been on Dr. Anderson's table. She lay back, testing the feel of it: hard.

A knock on the door. Dr. Barbash, a short plump woman with freckles, her hair in one long braid, entered. She sat on the stool at the end of the table, then walked its wheels closer, like a kid who'd outgrown her tricycle. She fumbled with some instruments in a metal tray.

Jana tensed as she felt the gloved finger enter. There was pain, but she had felt similar pain before: it was Ed's pain. The glove paused. Dr. Barbash told her to take a deep breath. She took a Pap smear, then reached for a different instrument and continued probing. Jana screamed. Dr. Barbash eased her way out. "Almost done now, stay there for one more moment."

She caught sight of the glove suspended in air and had to fight the temptation to reach out and fondle it. This was not Ed, Jana told herself—the doctor's hand might have entered her vaginal cavity, but it did not bask in her wetness. Instead it pulled a tissue from a gray, unmarked box and wiped her dry.

Dr. Barbash told her to get dressed, then come across the hall to her office. Jana found it uncomfortable to close her legs, hard to walk straight. The thick seam of her jeans rubbed painfully against her crotch.

"I suggest you continue using prophylactics for the time being," Dr. Barbash began. She explained that birth control pills had too many side effects once a woman turned thirty, and in Jana's case a diaphragm might cause needless pain. Apparently her vagina was "the size of a seventeen-year-old's."

"I feel an obstruction there, possibly a cyst," Dr. Barbash continued, "but I can't get close enough to tell precisely what it is. As your sex life increases, you'll be easier to examine. Meanwhile, let's wait and see if the Pap smear indicates any problems." She asked Jana to find out if her mother took DES during pregnancy, commenting that similar blockages were often found in DES babies. Smiling reassuringly, she ushered her new patient to the door.

ℰℐ ℰℐ

On the subway downtown, Jana struck upon the perfect image for the Artistic Response to the Environment exhibition: a series of inkblots. She'd title them "Vaginal Blockages: DES Babies." "No thinking about the environment exhibition today," she chided herself, closing her eyes in disgust. As Natalie continually reminded her, life at The Paperworks Space couldn't come to a halt simply because of the city-wide exhibition. They scheduled twelve six-week shows, two at a time, with three days between shows for taking one down and hanging the next. Life was always busiest during these interim periods.

The packer was putting the lids on three crates when Jana walked in. "The artist isn't going to be very happy about getting these back," Natalie mumbled.

"I know," Jana said. Those crates seemed larger and more imposing today than when they'd first arrived. "How many sold?"

"Two. And they were the cheapest works."

"Does he know yet?"

"Not unless you told him. Those details are your responsibility."

"I was trying to forget." Jana sat down and shoved paper in her typewriter. She banged out the artist's name, then tried to think what to say next. With most people, she could write "We're delighted to inform you that The Paperworks Space sold x number of drawings," but this guy wouldn't sit still for that. A native Georgian who had not previously shown in New York, he'd formed unrealistic expectations: All New York shows would be covered in every major arts magazine and sell out the first week. He'd already complained when *The Village Voice* was the only paper to review the show. He'd probably blame the insignificant sales on the gallery's poor management. For the first time this season, Jana made her yearly vow to exhibit only artists who displayed a professional outlook. Even as she made that promise, she glanced at the crates stacked against the far wall and wondered if the artists they'd begin hanging tomorrow would be any easier to work with.

"You've got to be more patient with people," Ed would say if he saw her now. In his job, in his life, in their life together, Ed was a living, breathing model of patience. "And look where it's gotten us," Jana thought angrily, pressing her hand to her stomach.

❧ ❧

Ed massaged her clitoris, still sore from the doctor's probing. "I always thought I ought to be a doctor," he told her.

"You would have made a wonderful doctor."

"When I was four years old, my aunt gave me a doctor kit for Christmas. I went around for weeks treating everyone in the family. I used up the candy pills, so they gave me jelly beans to put in the bottle. I still remember: the white ones were for headaches, the yellow ones were for fever, the pink ones were for upset stomachs. My cousin kept faking sick because he wanted candy, but I fixed him good—I gave him shots instead."

Ed moved his fingers gently while he talked, recalling how those nights when his mother returned from the doctor were the hardest. Usually the doctors—one after another—could find no physical cause for her symptoms, and she would get depressed and lie in bed for days. "My mother told me I was better than those insensitive doctors who treated her," he said out loud. "She taught me to dab the skin with alcohol before giving a shot. She taught me to warm the stethoscope in my hands before I held it against her. I was so proud." He kissed Jana's chest.

Jana felt her body tense. It seemed as if every time Ed touched her in some new way, it sparked some vague, hazy feeling of shame. She guided his hand stiffly back to her crotch. "Harder, please."

"Not tonight, dear." He rubbed more and more gently, easing the sensation until it vanished. "You've been through too much today," he told her. "But I wanted you to realize your body could still yearn to be touched, even after that doctor."

"Even after that doctor." She repeated Ed's words to herself, gradually drawing the image into focus. *That doctor* told her he would ease her stomachache. He led her into his small, narrow room in the camp's infirmary. She closed her eyes and remembered his warmth against her, then buried her head in Ed's chest to suppress the image.

"Tomorrow," Ed whispered. "Tomorrow."

❧ ❧

"I'm not a doctor," Ed mumbled as he was about to drift off to sleep.

Jana reached out an arm and let it rest on Ed's nipple. "I know that," she whispered. She saw herself clearly now, lying on top of the bleached white sheets and the thin green wool blanket that made her itch, while the doctor towered above her. He was telling her the counselors suspected that she was faking sick. "The kids hate me," she was crying. "If you send me back to my bunk they'll start teasing me again."

"Nobody hates you," he assured her between kisses. He worked his way lower. "Besides, if things get too bad, you can always come back here. You'll always be welcome here." *Tomorrow,* Ed had whispered, *tomorrow.*

"I can't help being afraid," she told Ed. "I still expect you to tell me I have to go back to my apartment tomorrow. You'll say the neighbors are starting to get suspicious because I'm here all the time. Like he did."

"Like who?"

Jana sat up in bed, trembling. She'd certainly been thinking about that experience a lot lately, but she hadn't planned on telling Ed about it, not yet. The words just slipped out. She stared out the window at the blue haze coming from someone's TV set across the street. "A doctor who treated me when I went away to camp," she said finally, and for the first time in years, she spoke his name: "Dr. Waters."

Ed rubbed the sleep out of his eyes. He tried to press her close, but she pulled away. "I was ten years old," she continued as if speaking from a trance. "I had no friends at home. I thought if I got around new people, some place where no one knew me, all the kids would like me. I pleaded to go to camp in the Catskills, but even there nobody wanted to be my friend. Then I started developing stomachaches. Dr. Waters kept me in the infirmary overnight, as a precautionary measure. My stomach started hurting again late that night, when there was no one around. He assured me he wasn't going to make me drink more medicine, that he knew another way to soothe the pain. Then he took me into his room and kissed me—low, around my crotch. I developed chronic stomachaches and spent a lot of nights in the infirmary that summer. Whenever no one else was around, he'd take me into his room, lay me on his bed, pull down my pajamas, and kiss my tummy."

"So that's what it was," Ed mumbled. "I knew there had to be something in your past to make you so afraid." Gently he rubbed her back. "I love you," he whispered. "I love you and if I want to hug you or kiss you it's only because I love you. I care about what happens to you. That's the difference between me and that doctor."

Jana clung to his body as if trying to rob it of all its strength. "Sometimes it's hard to believe how much you care," she told him. "Or when I do, it frightens me."

"I know, dear. And I'm not going to pretend there won't be emotional consequences. It's never easy to care about another person, but as long as we love each other, I want you here with me. Sometimes it feels as if I'm going to want you here always." He wanted to hold her tighter, kiss her all over her body, kiss her stomach, kiss her crotch, make the hurt of every doctor go away. Instead he sucked her breast.

That first night, last summer, she'd enjoyed it immensely when Ed cupped her breast in his soft, warm hand. Later she'd sat by the window at Yaddo and tried to play with her breast herself. But it was different now, he sucked like an infant, her nipples grew hard, and a sensation started in the upper half of her body that felt inappropriate, *dirty*. "Ed," she said, cautiously, "you can kiss me, uh, *lower down* if you want." Maybe he would just rub her there. She would love it if he'd massage her clitoris, like he'd done earlier tonight. Get the sensation back in the right place, make it strong enough, then maybe she'd be able to tolerate the rest.

Neither his hand nor his mouth moved.

"You're not some seventy-year-old doctor," Jana continued. "I know that now, and I want to be able to prove it—to prove how much I love you." *Don't you feel a little bit loved?* Ed would often ask as he was fondling her. Was this really what love was? Last spring she'd frozen when he'd clasped her hand. Ed could take her hand now and she didn't back away. But holding her hand was a long way from intercourse. Maybe she'd end up frigid after all.

"I'm not that doctor. And you're not that little girl." Ed moved his hands slowly, gently down her body. He kissed along the crease her panties' waistband left, wet, warm. Then he kissed along a slightly lower line, then . . .

"No!" she cried. "Stop, please." Unable to control herself, she pushed his head away from her abdomen. Pushed as she'd never dared push Dr. Waters. "I'm sorry," she cried a moment later, drawing him back. "I thought I could, but I can't. Not yet. I'm sorry."

"Not to worry, dear. Not to worry." Holding her, he pictured that selfish bastard of a doctor: wife gone, kids grown, retired except for two months at a summer camp, thinks he's all alone in the world, picks on some innocent child, trying to recapture the validation he felt in honest relationships. "Pervert," Ed called him aloud. "All that mattered was his own gratification, as if your body was his God-given right. He never stopped to consider how harmful it would be for you."

"He didn't hurt me," Jana halfheartedly tried to argue.

"Yes he did, dear. I have a feeling he hurt you much more than you realize."

"It wasn't as if he raped me."

"Of course he raped you! You don't have to be penetrated to be sexually molested. The important thing is not what he did to you, but how the experience affected you." He thought about how confused she'd been by her wetness at first. And even before that, the way she'd stiffened that first time he'd touched her. Her warm body pressing against his that night she'd been so upset about the subway commission. The way she'd pressed against his chest earlier tonight even, pleading, as if his touch was the only thing in the world which could quiet her. That summer, Jana had been on the brink of adolescence, a time when children tend to exaggerate their emotions. For all Ed knew, that doctor might not have done anything. But there was no denying how painful the experience had been.

They lay silently, unstirring, for what seemed like hours. Jana's thoughts drifted back to the scene in Dr. Waters' narrow room—she'd been lying there, turning her attention to crickets outside the open window, a frog or two croaking from the pond down the hill. She'd known that what he was doing was wrong, yet she'd lain there pretending she didn't know.

She closed her eyes and tried to just be with Ed, the down comforter over them, flannel sheets beneath them. There's no place I'd rather be, she tried to tell herself. But there weren't any street noises, let alone crickets, to distract her from those memories. The quieter it got, the closer Dr. Waters loomed. "Maybe a drink will help me get to sleep," she said, getting out of bed.

"Here, I'll get it for you. We could both use a drink." Ed grabbed his robe and followed her into the kitchen. She already had a bottle of cognac on the table. Ed got two glasses and poured healthy shots.

They sat silently, drinking until the glasses were half-empty. "What you were doing *did* feel pleasurable," Jana said, looking up at him. "I think maybe that's what frightened me." *Cling to me,* Ed had said those first times she'd been frightened by his advances, *cling to me.*

"I know."

"No, you don't know. Not this time." Jana set her glass heavily on the table. "It's hard to explain, but I think the pleasure I was feeling might have been familiar. Maybe I felt it with Dr. Waters, too. Maybe his kissing my stomach might not have been so terribly wrong." He wasn't doing anything to me that you weren't trying to do, she wanted to scream. If Dr. Waters was wrong, then you were wrong, too.

"What he was doing was wrong," Ed assured her.

She flashed on Sharma sitting at the table when they'd had dinner with Marilyn and Andy last week. The lace collar of Sharma's blouse had fallen open across her newly formed breasts. She had beautiful, firm breasts but wore them on a child's body, with no awareness of their power. And Sharma was thirteen, three years older than Jana had been that year she went away to camp. Was it any wonder she'd been so confused by Dr. Waters?

Sharma might be too young now, but by the time someone like Ed came along to fondle those breasts, you could be certain her mother would have explained the experience to her. Sharma would never feel guilty if her body responded, responded . . . Responded how? Jana wanted to say *normally.*

Sharma wasn't here. Marilyn wasn't here. Dr. Waters would only be here if she let him in. The dim fluorescent light hummed and flickered over the counter, reminding her that Ed was the only person in the room with her. There was nothing to be afraid of. If Jana could say the words, all the fear would vanish. "The only thing that was wrong, perhaps, was that I was too insecure to trust my enjoyment. Maybe it was a form of self-punishment: mentally I was pleading with my parents, 'Take me out of camp, even though I haven't told you what happened, and I promise never to enjoy being touched or kissed again.' Is such a thing possible?"

Ed slid his chair back. Stared at her. Suddenly her face became grained with age. Her jaw seemed to move on its own, like a Charlie McCarthy puppet. "Well, he started it, with his 'don't ever tell anyone about what we do here.' How was I supposed to react? He frightened me. And I was even more frightened, I think, because I enjoyed the experience, while he was hinting that it was forbidden."

Ed stood behind her now, gently massaging her shoulders. "Hey, take it easy. It's all right to realize that." He bent over and pressed his cheek against hers. "Everything's okay now. I'm not that doctor." Hugging her, feeling her close to him, made her real again. "You're upset today, that's all," he continued softly. "You're still feeling the effects of Dr. Barbash's examination. I know how hard it must be for you. Honest, I know."

Jana was on her feet, returning his hug, letting her body make itself small in the folds of her lover's. This was the comfort she had wanted from her parents, making the world right again. But she'd never even let them know what happened.

c/∂ c/∂

Jana massaged both temples at once with a paint-stained hand, then drew her fingers slowly and firmly along her forehead until they met in the center. She was working with oil, which meant she had to keep the windows open—ever since she started getting sinus headaches three years ago, she'd become sensitive to the fumes. She'd also fallen asleep with her head on Ed's chest last night, inhaling the stale odor of his cigarettes, which didn't help her sinuses any. It was too cold to think straight, but she kept layering colors on the painting in front of her, determined to torture herself.

A postcard of Matisse's *Odalisque with Magnolias* was tacked to the top of her easel, and Jana had spent the past two days trying to merge those lines with her mirror-image. "I'll bet a woman that large would be easy for Dr. Barbash to examine," she thought wryly as she extended the stomach curve. Oh, screw it! She'd tacked that postcard up to remind her of Ed's grace, not to torment herself with fat-woman imagery. But there was no use kidding herself—if Ed had been fat when she'd met him, she'd probably have used his physique as an excuse to reject him.

She'd been trying to convince herself that Ed's caring was enough to carry her through all her fears, including the suddenly resurfacing memories of Dr. Waters. Now it seemed as if the longer they were together, the more frightened she was becoming. Frightened by what Dr. Waters had done to her body years ago. Frightened by the blockage discovered in her vaginal tract only yesterday. Well, at least there was something that could be done about the present—alleviation, answers, could be as close as the paint-specked telephone.

"I don't remember, Jan," her mother said. "That was a long time ago. I told the doctor I didn't want to hear the details, I just wanted to have the child. It was a difficult pregnancy. You were supposed to be a cesarean, they didn't think I could carry you full-term, but you came out before they were expecting you."

"But Mom, if you used DES, they *must* have told you. I went to a gynecologist, and she discovered a blockage in my vaginal tract. She can't explain it, but there's a good chance it was caused by DES."

Her mother gasped, then asked if she was in much pain.

"I'm feeling fine. There's a mucous discharge, but they tell me that's to be expected." To be expected when a woman becomes sexually active, she added silently.

"Well, you must have been having problems if you went to a doctor."

Jana braced herself. She knew it would come to this—if she called her parents to ask about the DES, she would have to explain about Ed. Frantically she tried to think of the proper words. Dr. Barbash had explained that gynecological problems aren't only found in people who are sexually active, but she'd just told her mother she was feeling fine. She lowered her voice as if they were finally sharing a secret. "I wanted birth control pills," she stated flatly. She stopped herself before she said the rest, that she couldn't get the pills because she was too old now.

"Be careful," her mother whispered after what seemed an interminable silence.

"We are, don't worry."

"When are you going back to the doctor?"

"She'll have the results of the Pap smear next week. If it doesn't indicate any problems, she wants me to make an appointment in a few weeks."

"You'll call me as soon as you know anything?"

"I will, I promise." Jana pressed the phone to her ear—her mother wanted to know this time. Everything was turning out differently than she'd expected. There was no screaming, no tantrums, only adults caring about each other. It was almost like speaking with Ed.

"You don't think you'd rather come home?" her mother asked. "You'd probably feel better if you could rest and let someone take care of you for a while."

"Ed's here," Jana heard herself saying. "I just wish it were easier for me to accept being cared for. I'm finding it difficult to make a commitment to another person, even when I'm feeling good," she continued, slowly. Could Marilyn have been right? Was it possible her parents had done something to make her not only ashamed, but *afraid* of sex?

"I always wanted to do everything on my own, too. Everyone thought I'd never get married," her mother said. "Pop liked to call Daddy 'Last Chance Replance.'"

"You never slept with anyone before you were married, did you, Mom?" Jana made it sound as if she were joking.

"Not on your life." Her mother went on to talk about Marty, a guy she'd dated when she'd lived in Chicago. Her roommate was dating a close friend of Marty's, and it was arranged that they'd all go to a movie. When they came back to the apartment afterwards, the other couple went into the bedroom and closed the door. "Finally it got late, and I told Marty I was tired. I asked him to please go get his friend so the two of them could leave. Poor Marty had to explain to me what they were doing in there. They obviously assumed we were doing the same."

Jana couldn't believe her ears. She'd never seen her mother this open or honest before. But she'd never steered the conversation in this direction either. "No guys ever forced the issue?" she asked.

"Never. Or if they started to, I was too innocent to know what was happening," her mother laughed.

"I know the feeling," Jana laughed back. But the laugh was cut short. She closed her eyes, sucked her breath in. She'd been desperate to talk to her mother about this—the talk with Ed had eased the desperation, but still... "Somebody forced himself on me once," she said, softly. "I never told you about that, did I?"

"What do you mean 'forced himself on you'?" her mother's voice rose a pitch. "When? What did he do to you?"

"Oh, not forced himself exactly—he kissed my stomach, around that area. When I was a child."

"It was that doctor, wasn't it? That doctor who took care of you at camp. What was his name White, Walt, Waters?"

Jana would have gasped if she could have gotten air from somewhere. She felt a hot flash, the kind her mother used to complain about. "Waters," she whispered. Then: "How did you know it was him?"

"I should have realized. I told your father at the time I suspected something. When am I going to learn to trust my instincts?"

"But how? What would have made you suspicious?"

"It just didn't seem right, you spending half the summer in the infirmary."

"Why didn't you say anything? Why didn't you ask me about it?"

"I didn't want to frighten you. You were a little withdrawn when you first came home, then school started and you seemed fine. I kept thinking that even if something had happened, if we didn't bring it up you'd forget about it."

"You never stopped to think that it might come back to haunt me later?"

"You seemed fine."

The phone appeared to go dead. Jana searched the silence for memories of her childhood, something to reassure herself that her parents had been looking out for her. She thought about how her mother would sit on the seesaw with her when no other kids were around, trying in vain to shift her weight so Jana could go up and down.

"I guess maybe I would have liked to talk to you about the experience, but I didn't know where to begin," her mother said, breaking the eerie silence. "You didn't have an understanding of right and wrong, sexually. If I'd tried to tell you to never let anyone touch your genitals or expose himself to you, and you'd already been subjected to that, you'd probably have thought I was blaming you."

"But, Mom didn't it ever dawn on you that I might have known it was wrong? Dr. Waters implied as much—he kept telling me how important it was to keep this our secret. You never realized I might have been blaming myself all these years?"

"No, I never realized that. Don't forget, you're talking about twenty-five years ago. It wasn't like it is today—sex simply wasn't discussed among the people we associated with." There was that interminable silence again, then: "Your father and I were doing what we thought was best."

"I know that," Jana said, half to herself. It wasn't anyone's fault that her parents hold different values than she does—at least this time they weren't attempting to impose them. They were all doing what they thought was best.

Until now, her parents had been the only ones to love her, and she had rejected their love as obligatory. Maybe, thanks to Ed, she was finally learning how to love them back. "I know that," Jana repeated. And if she stayed with Ed long enough, she might someday believe it.

CHAPTER EIGHT

Power and Light

"LOOK, MA, no hands," Ed teased, holding the tip of his cock against Jana's belly button, letting it peek inside. Night after night, she would lie on her back while he went to the bathroom to wash, fascinated by the pleasure she'd been able to give so easily. Now that he'd come, she could relax and let his fingers fulfill her, confident she had nothing more to fear tonight.

The longer she holds onto her virginity, the more afraid of losing it a woman becomes, Jana realized. The longer a woman holds onto her virginity, the more she learns to appreciate that love is more than sex, it's cuddling, sharing with another person, even doing dishes together: Ed's explanation.

"Take a good look around," Ed told his cock.

She reached out to playfully push his hand away, then edged quickly away from him. Ed followed. "I thought . . ." she managed.

"You thought exactly what I wanted you to think," he said, softly.

"I don't understand . . ."

"We have to, dear." He tried to place his cock against her again. Jana shielded herself with her hands, one clasped over the other. Ed heaved a sigh, rolled onto his back, and took her hand in his, pressing finger after finger gently as he talked. "I wish we didn't have to do this, dear. But we have to make you large enough for the doctor to examine you." He wrapped his arms around her. "We'll try again tomorrow night, okay?"

"Okay, I guess."

"And I might have to keep pushing my way in even if you protest, but it's only because I'm as concerned about that obstruction as your doctor is."

Jana sighed agreement. "I'll try not to hurt you," he whispered, his arms grasping her so tightly that he was hurting her even now.

From that night on they approached the problem together, more rational than passionate. First he used his fingers to get her stimulated. Then he slipped into what they laughingly referred to as his "raincoat." He learned to open the foil pack with his teeth and put the rubber on single-handedly. Jana fought to keep her legs raised a little longer, a little higher. They tried a pillow under her lower back, then two pillows. He was certain it would be easier if he could just find the right angle.

Twice they thought he might have broken through, but when she ran to the bathroom to check, she found no blood. Then the next night they would get in bed full of expectation, only to discover she was tighter than ever. Until at last, on a night not that different from all other nights, the evening of a day when he'd gotten up late and run out of the house so quickly that he didn't take her in his arms for even a quick hug, he got through: October 14, 1984, two days after her parents' anniversary. The pain was less than she had expected—less than last summer when her body had been pushed into new positions, or last month when she felt as if she'd been horseback riding and walked with her legs apart for days on end.

They had a bottle of champagne in the icebox; Ed bought it last summer and had been saving it for this occasion. The cork flew off, hitting the ceiling and landing in the middle of the bed. Giggling to cover their sudden foreignness with each other, they crawled in after it, clinked their glasses, and sat up drinking, hugging. Finally, at three AM they turned the lamp off. Just tonight, Ed wanted to sleep with his arms around her, but Jana still had a hard time getting comfortable when he was that close, and they both needed as much rest as they could get.

℘ ℘

"Being with Ed hasn't improved my timing any," Jana thought dryly as she arranged miniature Danish on a silver tray. "Leave it to me to lose my virginity the night before a board meeting." All the meetings with APL were taking their toll on her, but there was no reason she should be nervous before a meeting of The Paperworks Space board. She knew these ten people well, some were old friends, all unquestionably supported the gallery. She popped a Danish into her mouth, walked over and set the tray on the center of the table, then sat down.

"I assume everyone received copies of the budget Associated Power and Light has planned for the forthcoming exhibition," Natalie said as she opened the meeting. "As most of you know, it's quite a bit more than we originally budgeted. Obviously, if APL wants to go all out with a gala reception, it's not our place to stop them. What I'd like is input from everyone on ways in which this extravagance can work to the benefit of The Paperworks Space and the artists involved in the exhibition."

When no one else spoke up immediately, Gary Jeffreys began. "Sidestepping the gala a bit, I'm more interested in the $31,500 figure for promotion costs," he said. "APL obviously wants to publicize the exhibition for the exposure they'll get as sponsors, but there are various ways that can be handled. If we're talking in terms of helping the artists benefit from all the promo, then the first order of business might be to insist that all eighteen artists be mentioned on advertising and promotional material."

"If they list eighteen names, plus six sites, and the exhibition's title, isn't that going to mean more text than the eye can take in at once?" Bill Fitch asked. "I would hope the ad designs would be as aesthetically pleasing as the drawings themselves are."

"The list can be printed in undiluted ink on major ads and in a screen tint as background for ads with less available space. That process paces the viewer's impressions, so not all the information jumps out at him," Gary pointed out. He and Larry Rivers were the two working artists on their board, selected for the purpose of protecting artistic interests. Gary, put on two years ago, had been Jana's suggestion, and at the moment she was proud of that decision.

"We have to remember how insistent APL was that we include bigname draws. I want to be certain these artists don't get undue attention," Jana said.

"More than likely those names will be listed first, but frankly I see that as working to our benefit as well," Bill said. "If the other names are listed randomly instead of alphabetically, no one is likely to notice any discrimination. If the media wants to focus on the larger names, then there's not very much we can do about that."

"Anything which draws people to the show is fine with me," Natalie said. "Besides, APL's promo department went out of their way to get detailed background info on *all* the artists and plans to deluge the various hometown newspapers. Color stories in those papers will soften the blow a bit if metropolitan coverage focuses on stars."

"My guess is Jana might have been referring to the 'big-name draws' bringing in the wrong kind of publicity," Gary said. Sitting next to Jana, he could sense her tensing as she'd made that statement.

Everyone in the room was silent, until finally Bill reminded them that they weren't dealing with Daniel Berrigan here. "People in the art world might be aware of Matt Fillmore's controversial pieces, but the media at large isn't likely to notice them. And we can be fairly certain APL's promotion department isn't going to highlight them on the press releases they send out."

The tension eased, but for Jana it was only momentary. The presidential election was in less than three weeks. Ed might be a registered Democrat, but he would be voting for Reagan this time around. Their relationship was new and exciting enough that they were able to avoid political issues at the moment; she hoped Matt Fillmore's work wouldn't force them into a confrontation.

Another board member, a vice president at one of the city's largest advertising agencies, offered to look over the stats of any advertisements before APL sent them into the papers, if Natalie could arrange it.

"We'll do our best," Natalie promised, casting a quick glance at Jana.

Jana ignored her boss. Unfortunately—or maybe it was fortunately—Ed never had much to say about the work he brought home with him. Jana had as much chance of seeing those photostats as Natalie did. "Strange things *do* happen," she thought. Two months ago she'd have said she had as much chance of seeing those stats as she did of losing her virginity.

⌘   ⌘

Gary hung around afterward and helped clean up. "Sorry to hear you didn't get the DCA commission," he said as they were clearing off the table.

"You win some, you lose some." Jana tried to laugh off the hurt of that commission. "I'm in a three-person show at Walker Art Center, as a result of someone seeing those slides at DCA. And there wasn't a thing Harriman could do about that."

"You think Harriman blocked the commission?"

"I'm certain he did. You know how he feels about me—forget the fact that I'm working in oil now, I could be making my own paints for all he cares. He's not about to give me any credit."

"Remember when you swore you'd never work with any paint which couldn't be easily washed off?" Gary teased.

"Even if I'd forgotten, I'm sure you'd remind me. Besides, you were working with encaustic, not oil. That's even more of a mess."

Jana had met Gary in Harriman's classes in 1970, and Gary made overtures of friendship from the start. One day she'd been in the area and dropped in at his studio. She found him in the middle of gluing bits of unbleached wool onto a black canvas. The black paint, the wool, and the encaustic stuck to his hands and completely covered his printer's apron. She'd vowed out loud never to let herself get that dirty. She couldn't see herself having the patience to give her body the scrubbing it would require after such a mess, art or no art.

"You've come a long way," Gary laughed.

"Longer than you know," she said, casting a smile in his direction which she hoped would convey most of what had happened over the past few months. Before Ed, Gary was the only person she'd ever tried to love. "You're too selfish to ever love anyone," Gary had written twelve years ago in a letter Jana still had around her apartment. Even Natalie had looked at it and said immediately: "He's just jealous because you got into a group show at Nancy Hoffman while he's off teaching in some godforsaken college to earn enough money to live on." Jana laughed to think of that conversation now. Had they all been so young and desperate once?

You're too selfish to ever love anyone. Those words juxtaposed in her mind with his words from the one night they'd spent together: "Trust me. I know you're afraid, but I won't let you down, I promise." After that, he'd gone into a stream-of-consciousness monologue, convinced that if he confided his every thought it would put her at ease. Gary's body felt hard, muscular, bony, as unsuited to hers as Ed's had been that first night he hugged her. They lay on his studio couch, Gary taking up most of the room, while she found herself huddled against a wall whose plaster, she noticed, badly needed patching. They didn't make love because she wasn't protected. Two weeks later Gary had taken the job in Wisconsin.

"We've *both* come a long way," she said, still smiling. Artistically speaking, Gary showed regularly at O.K. Harris, and had a one-man installation at PSI last year. Jana rinsed the last of the dishes and set them in the rack to dry, flicking her wet hands in his direction as once, sitting around her apartment years ago, he'd initiated a pillow fight.

e/> e/>

"Ed . . ." Ed rolled onto his back, sighed, reached down to his crotch. "What's wrong?" Jana sat up. "Something's wrong, I know it is."

He shook his head. "Wait. I'm not sure."

"It broke, didn't it?" The flat calmness of her tone amazed her.

"I think so."

Her eyes blinked but remained dry. She felt completely numb. Frigid. "I'm going to wash up," she said. She mainly wanted to get away from him. There had been no pain, only warmth. She realized what happened the moment his semen mixed with her own harmless wetness. She recalled the times he'd started to ejaculate before she withdrew her hand, the one time he couldn't move away quickly enough and accidentally came all over her stomach.

"Ed," she called from the bathroom, "does semen have blood in it?"

"What?"

"There's blood mixed in with the mucous."

Ed jumped up. The half-torn rubber dangled from his cock, then fell off. He grabbed her at the bathroom door and spun her around. "That means you've still got your period. If there's blood then you've still got your period," he sang. Jana pulled away. Her period seemed to have stopped three or four days ago. She looked again. There were definitely spots of blood on the white toilet paper folded like a Dear John letter in her hand. It reminded her of when she'd had the yeast infection.

Ed pushed past her into the bathroom, washed up, returned to bed, gave her one big hug, then turned over and tried to get to sleep. She lay staring at the dark window, thinking of jumping, but Ed's soft, warm body had positioned itself between her and the world outside. Was this what love was? She thought the world's problems would be solved the moment she lost her virginity.

No matter what position she lay in, her arm seemed to get in the way of the rest of her body. The further away sleep seemed, the more her thoughts wandered. She forced her eyes closed. Finally she managed to envision a fence before her, one of those fences made from twisted, knotty logs, the bark still clinging in places. At last the sheep began jumping over, their hind legs stretching out to clear the fence easily. When they got to the other side they lay in the pasture, lowering themselves front quarters first, like camels. She counted sixteen, seventeen, eighteen go over the fence and recline in that manner. As the count continued, the sheep's bodies took on less and less tension, until they appeared to be furry pillows carried by the wind. Thirty-four, thirty-five, thirty-six, Jana counted. Then it all trailed off to wherever sleeping sheep go.

છે   છે

"That's happened to a lot of couples," Natalie laughed. "I don't think you have anything to worry about—as long as Ed pulled out right away, the semen usually doesn't have time to penetrate. Besides, if worst comes to worst, you'll get an abortion." Natalie continued shifting two drawings around on the wall, as she'd been doing all afternoon, unable to decide which way they looked best. "Abortions are as common as colds these days. You won't have to go through what I went through twenty years ago, sneaking around, borrowing money, being picked up and dropped off on a street corner." She made it sound simple, but Jana had never even had her tonsils out. She'd known several women who'd had early, supposedly safe abortions and had been emotional wrecks for months afterward.

Ed didn't take things as lightly as Natalie did; he realized semen didn't need much encouragement to float up and impregnate a woman. But that was a chance women took. Most women could laugh about it, but Jana wasn't "most women." She'd overreacted to the rubber's breaking; if she was pregnant there was no telling what would happen. What the hell, he might not be thrilled at her neuroses, he might hope that in time she'd settle down, but he couldn't change her. The best he could do was try his best to alleviate her anxieties, hopefully without getting caught up in them himself.

He took off work early and picked her up at the gallery. They wandered around the Upper East Side in search of a new restaurant; as had become a habit when they were slightly tense, they channeled their energies into a spontaneous game. Tonight it involved finding a restaurant they hadn't eaten in before, complicated by geographical restrictions—the west side of Third Avenue, between 95th and 79th streets. The November air was still warm, and the walk was pleasant, but they wandered as far as 72nd Street without finding a restaurant that enticed them. Ed suggested they head back uptown, picking side streets between Second and Third avenues at random. At last, on 81st Street, they decided on a little place called Taverna España.

Jana took refuge in the secluded darkness. Her stomach was feeling queasy, but she didn't let that deter her from ordering a chorizo dish. They split a pitcher of sangria. Dinner was Ed's treat, his way of conveying he understood what she was going through. He was doing his best to block out the classical guitarist playing not more than twenty feet away from them, determined to give all his attention to her tonight, and making Jana feel guilty in the process. She recalled Milt Hinton playing at The Bottom Line two weeks ago, Ed tilting his head back in ecstasy, listening to the mysterious subtleties in the music which her ears were not attuned to. Thanks to Ed, she listened to more music than she might have a year ago, but her appreciation was still visually oriented—she was fascinated by Hinton's sheer physicality, the way he played as if he were making love to that bass. But the guitarist tonight might as well have been a statue. She stared at the bald spot Ed usually kept well covered; its exposure was the only indication that he hadn't slept well last night.

"I think it's time to call your doctor," Ed said between mouthfuls of paella, casually, as you would remind someone it was time to go to bed or time to turn on the seven o'clock news. "My guess is you'll be large enough for her to examine you now."

Jana detected a tinge of pleasure in his voice—the consequences might be disastrous, but he had gotten through; he had done what the doctor ordered. "I know," she said. She should have called Dr. Barbash a month ago, right after she'd lost her virginity. Only, what if she was still too small to be examined? She put down her fork. Sauce trickled down the sides of her mouth. She wiped it with her napkin, pressing the cloth hard against her face.

Ed resumed eating, chewing every mouthful ten times, the way his macrobiotic friends recommended. He suspected Jana was sitting there comparing herself to Kathe. He wanted to tell her how different she was, how Kathe would have made his life miserable for months afterward if she felt he hadn't taken enough precautions. But such a comment would only be playing up to Jana's neuroses, so he let it drop.

૯ઝ ૯ઝ

Once again Jana didn't sleep well. Her head was foggy the next morning, but she wasn't due at work until noon. She puttered around the apartment as long as she could, almost as if she had a premonition of trouble at the gallery. And sure enough, the first words out of Natalie's mouth were, "The slides of Matt Fillmore's work came this morning. I think you'd better have a look."

Jana flipped through the slides quickly, holding them up to the light and glancing at the titles. The piece entitled *Power and Light* was pretty hard to miss. She slid it into the projector and shone it on the office wall. In the foreground was a teepee bursting into flames, drawn with bold, vibrant red and brown strokes; inside the teepee an Indian family, bound and gagged, was depicted in a pen and ink drawing, while the background charcoal hinted at other Indians running in panic.

It took Jana a few minutes to remember: ten years ago the federal government had taken over land which belonged to the Seneca Nation. After leaving it vacant for seven years, they granted APL permission to use the land for a new generating plant. Work wasn't slated to begin on that plant for another two years yet; only the politically well informed would recall the small news items that appeared three years ago. Certainly no one on their board had remembered. Leave it to Matt Fillmore.

Deciding the front room could stay vacant for a few minutes, Natalie joined her in the office. "It's one of his strongest drawings," Jana said.

"I have a feeling that fact is going to be lost on APL."

"At least it's not a dead coyote."

Natalie laughed, remembering. When the Central Park Zoo first closed for renovation last year, an environmental art exhibit was held there. No one from the Parks Department bothered to look over the works before the show opened: one artist had nailed a dead coyote on a cross, next to a sign that read "He died for your sins." It caused a furor at the time. Mothers came with their children, since the exhibit was at the zoo, then ended up dragging them away from the horrific image of the crucified coyote. Even *Newsweek* covered the story. "It's a wonder Central Park's willing to risk another exhibition," she commented.

"They probably said it could never happen again," Jana said with a bitter laugh.

"It's our job to see that it doesn't."

"I feel more like a dictator than a curator." The more she looked at Matt's drawing, the more she found herself identifying with the Indians' point of view. It had the effect of drawing viewers in, making them more than innocent bystanders. Turning away from it, she asked if Natalie had talked to Bill Fitch yet.

"No. I wanted you to see it first." And now that Jana had seen the drawing, they had run out of excuses. Natalie went back to the front room and picked up the phone.

"There's one thing I'm *not* about to do, and that's try to explain the corporate view of life to the same liberals who made it possible for women like me to have legal abortions," Jana thought as she put the slide back in its case. She wondered what position their board president would take on the abortion issue. How could you typecast a man who'd been married for fifteen years, had three children, a wife who stayed home all day, and a three-bedroom condo on Central Park West, yet let his hair grow well below the collar of his Italian suits, which he wore with style? Bill was as much of a puzzle to her as Frank Markowitz was. But he *was* the person who'd recommended Matt Fillmore in the first place.

"Reprieve!" Natalie exclaimed, coming into the back again. "Bill's out of town until Monday." While they both understood this would ultimately be a matter for the entire board's consideration, there seemed no question that they had to speak to their president first. "You can keep it under wraps, can't you, Jana? I mean, you're not going to let anything slip to Ed, are you?"

"Listen, it's easier for me that way, too," Jana said, flicking off the slide projector. She and Ed had enough to think about as it was.

CHAPTER NINE

I Can't Say I Wasn't Concerned

FIRST THINGS FIRST: she wasn't pregnant. But the blood hadn't been from her period, either. Quite possibly, Jana was still bleeding a bit from having recently lost her virginity. Dr. Barbash suspected that as her lover reached into new areas, he might be causing slight abrasions. It was probably nothing to worry about, but she examined Jana with an electron microscope just to be sure. The magnification such an instrument provided would also give more insight into that "blockage."

"No sex for seventy-two hours," Dr. Barbash cautioned when Jana was dressed and sitting in her office. "I took a biopsy. You have an open wound there. It's very important that you give it time to heal."

Jana welcomed such an ordinance. Lately it was painful every time Ed touched her. Last night she'd tried but failed to repress her scream. "I had the wrong angle," Ed mumbled apologetically. He shifted his position but still seemed to be pushing against a bone.

She took his hand and guided it toward a pimple. "I'm a little sore there, see?"

"But look at how wet you are," Ed said, settling back on his own pillow. Wet, but passive. Sometimes he wished he didn't have to be the initiator all the time, but he supposed he couldn't ask for everything. He'd been with women before who had tried all kinds of kinky sex, and frankly, he found Jana's innocence more enjoyable than all of them put together.

Jana had never bothered to explain she was wet because of the mucous secretion around the suspicious blockage—Dr. Barbash remarked on her first examination that she was wetter than normal there. Jana had known for weeks it had nothing to do with how sexually excited she was. She resented the fact that he turned over and went to sleep easily, while she lay awake. She resented how much he enjoyed being with her, while she, she . . . Damn it, say the words: *she froze when he touched her.* "I'm not frigid, I'm frightened," she'd reminded herself as she sat in Dr. Barbash's office this morning.

"The blockage is caused by fibroid tumors," Dr. Barbash said, drawing Jana's attention back to the situation at hand. "I also found three or four minuscule warts, but I don't think they're anything to worry about. That's why I took a biopsy." She tapped the bottle in front of her. "I'll run this through the laboratory. Give me a call on Tuesday or Wednesday."

Jana wasn't feeling as shaky as she'd anticipated—Dr. Barbash had sprayed her with novocaine, the examination hadn't even been painful. She supposed she might as well go into the gallery for a few hours. She was halfway to the subway when she had a better idea. Stopping at a pay phone, she gave Natalie a call. "Look, if there's nothing urgent you need me for this afternoon, I might be better off going over to the library and seeing what information I can dig up on problems between artists and corporate sponsors. The more facts we have at our disposal when we talk to Bill, the easier it's going to be. And we need facts and figures, not hearsay."

Natalie agreed it sounded like a good idea, and Jana hailed a cab and went over to the main library at 42nd Street. Diego Rivera's Rockefeller Center mural was the most obvious example, so she started gathering information on that. "Think what a Rivera mural would be worth these days," she thought as she flipped through Rivera's biography. The hard copy confirmed her suspicions: Rockefeller knew Rivera was a communist; he knew the mural Henry Ford commissioned in Detroit had created a public scandal and was saved only through Edsel's intervention. Even when Rockefeller paid Rivera in full and prevented him from finishing the predominantly red mural with its distinct face of Lenin among the group of technicians in control of the universe, there was the promise that the work itself would be preserved. And what happened? Six months later construction crews entered the building at midnight and destroyed it. For years the wall remained blank, since no other artist was willing to paint over the wall that should have been Rivera's. Jana xeroxed the chapter talking about this mural, as well as information about Rivera's Detroit commission and his mural at the San Francisco Stock Exchange.

A passage in Rivera's biography led her to research José Clemente Orozco's work, which she found in a book on the Mexican Muralists. As if to make amends for the destruction of Rivera's Rockefeller Center mural, Nelson Rockefeller was instrumental in saving the mural criticizing higher education that Orozco did at Dartmouth. "Orozco saw it as his moral commitment to criticize his patrons," the description read. "Painting a mural for the Supreme Court in Mexico, he attacked the concept of justice. He always presented both sides of the issues, making people stop and sort things out for themselves." Jana highlighted this passage on her xerox, adding a note that Matt Fillmore was doing the same thing in his *Power and Light* drawing: making people stop and think. Fillmore wasn't trying to pull a fast one, either; he wasn't insisting upon working behind a curtain, as Rivera did in Detroit. No matter what the outcome, there would be no surprises in the forthcoming exhibition.

She had to look harder to find more recent examples of the corporate world interfering with art, but she eventually found them. In 1970, the University of Massachusetts took down Chuck Close's show because it included nudes; Close might have lost the case, but he fought hard, taking it as far as the Supreme Court. Jana chided herself for not having recalled that incident—no self-respecting artist had agreed to exhibit at U. Mass. since then. Searching further, she unearthed a brief newspaper article from the late sixties, relating that the Chicago and Vicinity Show had given a prize to a work which the officials at the museum of the Art Institute considered too obscene to exhibit. That story made her recall there being other incidents involving the Art Institute, and she prowled through various indices until she found references to the story of another artist whose construction depicted a couple having intercourse under the United States flag. Told he had to alter the piece if he wanted to be included in the show, he transformed the flag into a red and white striped blanket. The book where she found that story didn't bother to mention the artist's name. Perfect, Jana thought: the artists who sold out were the same ones whose names had long since been forgotten. This was exactly the sort of ammunition she wanted to feed their board.

She was on a roll now. Every reference she found pointed her toward the next, and before she knew it she'd xeroxed a dozen articles referring to ten different incidents. It was after seven o'clock before she realized what time it was. Meanwhile, Ed had come home early, concerned for her. She walked into the apartment to find that he'd become worried when he was unable to reach her at home and at the gallery. He'd changed into a sport shirt, opened a bottle of wine to let it breathe, and sat tensely waiting. He hugged her in silence, then, warned not to touch her in the one spot he could always be counted on to reach for first, he placed a gentle arm on her shoulder. His fingers lost their familiar playfulness. His concern for her made his palm sweaty as he approached her with an innocence that recalled their first nights together. Jana told herself he was looking out for her, trying to comfort her. But she needed love, not comfort.

༺ ༺

Bill's voice was calm and even: "I can't say I wasn't concerned about something like this happening." After making it clear the entire board had shared his concern, Jana told him about the research she'd done. "Sounds like you're off to a good start," he said. He glanced at his calendar; unfortunately, he was tied up with meetings all this week, and then was going to his wife's parents' in Virginia for Thanksgiving.

"My guess is other board members will find themselves with similar schedules," he continued. "Right before the holidays is difficult for everyone. Why don't you send me over copies of those articles, get in touch with the other board members, and arrange a meeting for the week after Thanksgiving? That will give us all time to consider our options." Jana and Natalie were only too happy to delay things another two weeks. Catalog copy wasn't due at the typesetter's until the end of January—they told themselves there would be plenty of time. Even so, Jana would be relieved when the whole board got involved in this mess; doing research over the past few days, she felt as if she'd been collecting stones to hurl at Ed.

Dr. Barbash wasn't in when Jana called on Tuesday. When Dr. Barbash returned the call, Jana was out. It went back and forth all week. Jana didn't want to speak with her from work, with Natalie and whoever else was in the gallery overhearing every word, so she left only her home number and Ed's number. Finally on Tuesday morning, two days before Thanksgiving, they connected.

"There's one thing I think you'll be pleased to hear," Dr. Barbash began. "You don't have to worry about birth control for the moment—those fibroids are in your uterine tract, blocking your tubes. It's nothing to worry about—over 20 percent of women of child-bearing age develop them. I'm actually not surprised, in your case. As I said, I think we can leave them alone for now. If you ever want children, they'd have to be surgically removed.

"What concerns me more are those warts," she continued. "It looks like you have a sexually transmitted wart virus, related to the herpes virus. I'd suggest you have your lover checked out. He might not develop symptoms for another six months, but he'd only reinfect you. You can be successfully treated in the morning and develop them again the same night." Dr. Barbash's voice sounded harsh and final—there's nothing more to discuss; don't bother me with idiotic questions.

"Wait a second, what about *me;* how are you going to cure the wart virus in me?" It wasn't until she'd hung up the phone that Jana realized she'd forgotten to ask.

She walked to the subway quickly and was out of breath by the time she got there. She broke out in a cold sweat. There you go, she thought: the first stages of sickness, the body weakened, subjected to common flu germs. She wasn't the sort of person who caught a cold easily, but when she did it would take her weeks, sometimes months, to knock it out of her system.

"Late night?" Natalie asked the minute she walked in.

"No. I'm catching a cold or something."

"You look awful."

"Thanks." Jana sat down and opened the folder containing preliminary catalog copy on the artists at the Central Park boat house. Not knowing what the next month would bring, she wanted to get a head start on any work she could. Picking up a pencil, she began making minor changes, shortening sentences, adding a descriptive word here and there, but mostly just shuffling papers.

"You're not much use today, are you?" Natalie stated gently, standing over Jana's desk forty minutes later and watching her curator staring off into space. "Why don't you go home and get to bed? The last thing we need is for you to take sick."

"Okay, okay, I'm going. You don't have to tell me twice today."

"Go home, crawl into bed, make some hot tea with a lot of lemon—or better yet, get some rosehip tea. Rosehips are a natural source of vitamin C, you know. And get Ed to nurse you for a few days—that's one of the advantages of living with someone."

Jana felt a chill run through her entire being. Leave it to Natalie. If she'd just left well enough alone, told her to take off early, she could probably have gone back to Ed's and enjoyed being nursed without thinking twice about it. But Natalie had managed to make it sound as if it was her feminine duty to accept Ed's nurturing, and the last thing she wanted to be right now was a woman.

She had no right to infect Ed with a cold, let alone a wart virus. But maybe she could put off telling him what the doctor said for a day or two. He certainly wouldn't want her to have sex with him when she was feeling so miserable—the infection wasn't about to spread any further tonight.

Walking a few blocks to get air, Jana thought about the other warts, moles, and birthmarks on her body. The largest one was on her neck. She vividly remembered being eight or nine years old, but small enough to be propped up on the special seat at the beauty parlor. She wanted a pixie cut, like the other kids had, and a lipsticked hairdresser with long unbitten fingernails was pulling her hair back and sarcastically asking her mother if they wanted that mole to show. "She should *never* wear her hair above her shoulders." It was as if Jana wasn't in the room.

She'd gotten her pixie cut by the time she'd gone away to camp, though. Dr. Waters never seemed to care about her mole. Now suddenly Ed cared; Ed cared too much, perhaps. Life had certainly been simpler when there was only herself to think about. Simpler, not better, Jana corrected herself.

℘ ℘

Jana lay with her eyes open: Ed was dressing as quietly as he could. She watched him reknot his blue paisley tie three times before he was satisfied. He looked so innocent, so unsuspecting that a wart virus might at this very moment be spreading through his system. Was this the time to tell him? She propped her head up on her arm. "Do you mind if I stay here today?" she asked. "I already warned Natalie not to expect me at the gallery, and I dread the thought of going across town to my place."

"Stay wherever you'll be most comfortable." He bent to kiss her, then remembered she was sick and kissed her forehead. Her sweaty arms clung to his freshly laundered shirt.

Climbing out of bed maybe an hour later, she rummaged through her pocketbook and pulled out *Ballet Girl,* a teenage romance novel she'd hurriedly thrown in there when she'd stopped at her apartment yesterday. Back in the old days, before Ed, these books had been as much a part of her life as pajamas with feet were. She'd learned from them what it meant to care for another person; she'd learned how not to be put off by gentle touch. Boys and girls held hands, and if the boy's hand wandered the girl drew away. Writers like Beverly Cleary or Norma Klein would describe two characters hugging, but there were never any indications of how tightly they hugged. They made it seem simple. The one thing none of them mentioned was that bodies might end up wanting more than touch.

Exactly seventy-two minutes after she'd sprawled out on the couch, a cup of tea with lemon cooling next to her, she read the last page. It was only a coincidence, she told herself; she hadn't even read the cover blurb. And yet the book closely paralleled her own situation—the fear of doctors, real illness bordering on hypochondria. The protagonist states that she'll never have children, since childbirth is painful. She nearly faints during a film portraying the beauty of natural childbirth. Jana got nauseated reading the description of the film. Back in grammar school, she used to throw up when they showed pictures of the body's organs during health class.

The book's ending was simplistic: the protagonist quits ballet school, hides out for a week in her father's attic, then all of the sudden she's healthy. She takes a walk around the block, comes back carrying her suitcase as if she's decided to visit her father unexpectedly. The next fall she goes off to college and lives in a coed dorm like a perfectly normal, well-adjusted teenager.

That's the difference, Jana thought—in real life, things don't work out so well. Ed's apartment wasn't an attic and there was no point in trying to hide. She decided to walk over to Shakespeare and Co. and find something more intelligent to read.

Standing before half a wall full of health and nutrition books, she glanced past *Let's Eat Right to Keep Fit,* past *Headaches and Health.* The ones she wanted had been pushed to the back of the shelves, covered by the more popular books. At last she unearthed some books which listed "genital warts" in their indices. The information was sketchy, though; the one thing all the books agreed on was that wart viruses were extremely difficult to treat thoroughly, and tended to recur. "Your lover would only reinfect you," Dr. Barbash said. "Scientists assume they are caused by a virus similar to that which causes warts on the hand," she read. Two books on women's hygiene mentioned the importance of washing and drying thoroughly after intercourse. "Oh great," Jana muttered. She washed sometimes, but many nights she was so tired she rolled right over and went to sleep.

Feeling suddenly faint, she bought three books, paid for them with her Visa card, hugged them to her chest as if they were an awkward stuffed animal, and caught a cab back to Ed's. She plopped down on the couch and opened the first book, which began with an illustrated description of the genitalia in men's and women's bodies. She picked up a pencil and doodled while she read, extending the man's limp penis, rounding out his chest. On a sketch of the woman's crotch she drew a plump hand, the cupped fingers with their finely shaped nails a fraction of an inch away from touching it.

No! What did she think she could do, show Ed this drawing and expect him to imagine the conflicting emotions she felt every time he touched her? She needed to understand whatever was going on inside her, not transform it. She tossed the pencil across the room, sat back and read slowly, absorbing every word into her body until the fever broke and she sat there almost catatonic.

"There's no use pretending I'm still gathering facts at the library," Jana realized, coming out of her trance. These books could only give general information, and what she needed were specifics about her *own* case. The more specifics she knew, the easier it would be to explain to Ed.

She knew what Ed would do if he were her. He'd do what any intelligent adult would do: call the doctor back. He would make himself a list of questions he wanted Dr. Barbash to answer: how could she have gotten the virus if it wasn't sexually transmitted? What else could it be? Could these be simple warts on her genitals, like she had on the rest of her body? If she loved Ed, then she had to make herself behave the way he would want her to.

"I said the infection *looks* like a wart virus. I'm not going to rule out other possibilities. They could be normal, uninfectious warts. I've discovered warts in other patients whose mothers took DES, and the cell changes looked almost identical. Wart virus is the logical assumption, and we're safest to treat it as such." Jana stressed how seldom they'd had intercourse, and Dr. Barbash explained that a wart virus could sometimes spread through rubbing the genital area, especially if the woman became stimulated. "Moisture aids the growth of warts," she added.

When Jana asked what sort of treatment she recommended, Dr. Barbash talked about burning it out. "That is, assuming it *is* a wart virus. I suggest we wait a month or two, then take another biopsy. If there are no further cell changes, then it's more than likely caused by the DES." She suggested Jana and Ed take precautions, but continue a normal sex life. "As your vagina enlarges you'll be easier to examine. It's important that all the warts be burnt out at the same time. Even after supposedly thorough treatment, the virus will be certain to recur if there are any that weren't spotted."

"I know. I was just reading about that in *Our Bodies, Our Selves.*"

"Then there's obviously nothing more you need me to tell you."

It took all Jana's energy to slam the phone down.

Ed would have kept Dr. Barbash on the phone until she'd explained everything. He would have asked her how dangerous the treatment was, what side effects it had. He would have inquired about other possible treatments. He would have found out how long treatment could be safely postponed. But she wasn't Ed. She needed Ed to hold her and talk to her. For a moment she even toyed with the idea of calling her parents. Not to torment them, not to throw it up to them the way she might have a few years ago, not to ask for their help even, just to have someone to talk to. Instead she folded her arms on the chair's arm, buried her head in her arms, and let the tears come out. There seemed to be no stopping them. She was terrified that she'd infect Ed with the wart virus. Terrified that if he found out about it he'd no longer love her.

She got up and washed the pile of dishes in the sink, trying to keep her mind occupied. Like most men, Ed usually stacked the dishes after eating, as if expecting them to wash and dry themselves. She finished the saucers and reached for one of the cups, taking care that lifting it wouldn't tumble the others. The sink was small, and there wasn't another basin to rinse things in. On top of that the drain had been clogged for the last two weeks and Ed insisted upon waiting for the super to fix it, which seemed to be taking forever. Maybe she'd have been better off going back to her apartment after all.

છ્ર છ્ર

Usually Ed was home by seven, seven-thirty at the latest. By six-thirty Jana was working herself into a frenzy practicing the words she would say when he arrived: "Ed, sweetheart, I'm scared for you. There's a good chance you have a wart virus." Way too direct; she didn't want to send him into a panic. "Would you believe it, we've killed ourselves taking precautions against pregnancy, and all for nothing. You'll never guess what Dr. Barbash found." No, that was too casual, like her father returning from a business trip, hiding a present behind his back. She gave up and rehearsed Ed's possible reactions—anger, concern, fear, confusion—and how she would try to respond to each one calmly, lovingly. She went over their hypothetical conversations so many times in her congested mind that whatever happened had to be a letdown. Fantasy was phasing out reality.

Tonight of all nights, Ed didn't get home until 8:15. And he was the one who spoke first. "I thought I'd never get out of the office. The whole secretarial staff left early for the holiday, and I had to go hunt down everything I needed to finish a few jobs. Then the trains were stalled, and I had to change over to the AA at Columbus Circle." Ed flipped through the mail she'd placed on the coffee table. "Do you feel like eating?" he asked distractedly. "Why don't we walk over to Victor's? I've been dreaming about their veal piccata all week."

They might as well eat, she supposed. Food was the easiest way for Ed to share with others—she couldn't match his interest in music, but at least she ought to share his love for long, quiet dinners. If they relaxed a bit together she might find it easier to tell him what was going on. Victor's had a pianist Ed enjoyed immensely, the music might act as a buffer. When he was listening to music, Ed's usual edge of tension seemed to vanish.

They arrived to discover Victor had given the pianist the night off; there was only the candlelight to set an atmosphere. Jana found herself counting the checks on the red-checked tablecloth. Was this the level their relationship had sunk to—she could sit through dinner, avoiding anything that mattered, and Ed would ramble on about things that happened at work?

"I talked to my secretary, and she agreed to send out the advance copies of the exhibition catalog," he began. "You've been pushing yourself pretty hard lately, and you still have that show in Minneapolis to prepare for." Sending out catalogs didn't require a curator's expertise, Ed realized. Much as he wanted to ease Jana's work load, he knew her self-esteem relied upon her professional responsibilities.

"That'll help. Thanks," Jana mumbled, thinking more about the wart virus. But when she was able to push medical concerns from her mind for a moment, her thoughts drifted to *Power and Light*.

"Phyllis agreed her staff can easily pick up the catalogs from the printer and see to it copies are distributed to the six locations well before the show opens. She was also wondering if you and Natalie had a particular photographer you wanted to use for the gala, or if you wanted her to hire someone?"

"Natalie should have the names and phone numbers of photographers we've hired for other openings. But I can't say there was anyone we were exactly thrilled with. To tell the truth, I haven't given it much thought; the exhibition's still six months away."

"Phyllis suspected as much. Most of the best people are booked at least four months in advance, so she wants to get started on it now. She said to assure you she's worked with some top people; if it's okay with you and Natalie, she'll make some calls to see who's available and take it from there. *The Times* is considering a feature on the exhibition in their Sunday supplement, by the way."

"He doesn't even notice I'm not eating," Jana thought bitterly. She pushed the food around on her plate and wondered if she was becoming anorexic, like she'd been at fifteen. She recalled those early days of their relationship, when she had played with her vegetables while he ate heartily. It had been a sign of progress, a mark of how comfortable she finally felt with Ed, when she could eat normally. Ed asked the waiter for a second cup of coffee while she stirred her now cold tea with brandy for the hundredth time. Tea with Courvoisier; Ed insisted on what he considered the best for her, his treat tonight.

At last they started walking home. She linked her arm in his. "I got through to Dr. Barbash," she began.

Ed stopped walking, turned to face her under a streetlight. He broke out in a grin she'd have thought he'd be too tired to manage. Before another word was said they started walking again, arms around each others' waists for support, more like drunks than lovers. She let her fingers play with a thread dangling from his tweed jacket.

"What did the doctor have to say?" he asked as they turned the corner and approached the entrance to his building. His voice was concerned but not anxious. There had been too much tension the past few weeks, with him irritated that she hadn't spoken to the doctor yet, and Jana disturbed by his impatience.

"Well, I have fibroid tumors, for one thing."

Ed stood motionless at her side, caught off-guard by the word *tumor*. Step by step she led him forward, the way you'd lead a frightened animal: one foot firmly in front of the other, no sudden movements. She rubbed her fingers gently along his backbone while he unlocked the apartment.

Once they were inside, Ed drew her close and held her, rocking back and forth. It was the same motion he used to get her stimulated, way back when she was still a virgin. "They're nothing to worry about, Dr. Barbash says," she began, trying to keep her attention on what she was saying. Ed's touch itself was torture; she had to fight hard to keep her body from wanting him. But he wouldn't let go of her. Softly, almost swallowing the words, she said "I love you."

"Time to get you to bed," Ed declared, still hugging her, leading her. "Sounds like you've had a hard day."

He helped her undress, like a good nurse, his large hands fumbling with each button. Softly, almost innocently, his fleshy palms brushed against her neck, her chest, her breasts. He folded her blouse and jeans and placed them on top of the dresser. Her panties, bra, and socks were in a heap on the floor, the way he left his own underwear. Then, having second thoughts, he picked them up and put them on top of her other things. Jana crawled into bed; Ed pulled the sheet and blanket over her, tucked one side under the mattress. "Do you think you'll be warm enough? I can get the quilt out of the closet . . ."

"I'll be fine." She stopped just short of reminding him that she could get up and get the quilt herself if she got cold later. She was half expecting him to offer to leave the light on, in case she woke up and was afraid of the dark. He'd done that for Kathe, hadn't he?

She swallowed hard, tasting the salt of her tears. The covers held her in, tightly, warmly. She wanted to drift off to sleep, saving the rest of her story until tomorrow, next week, next year. But Ed slipped into bed beside her. Suddenly she felt herself pressed against his sweaty skin. The hairs on his arms prickled. "When are you going back to the doctor?" he was asking already.

"I don't know exactly. Dr. Barbash says I'll be easier to treat if we wait a little longer." And this man, this animal next to her, was supposed to make her vagina larger. He didn't even realize the tumors were best left alone, that the "treatment" Dr. Barbash recommended was for a wart virus, a *contagious* wart virus. Jana turned her head away. Sickness made her dependent on him again. It made her helpless, if not one way, then another. Well, she wasn't about to submit to it. With any luck, by tomorrow night she'd be back home sleeping in her own bed, maybe with the lion's head squeezed between her thighs, hurting him.

No, she wouldn't. Whatever she was going through, it wasn't Ed's fault. He was concerned for her and, as long as she had chosen to lie here next to him, she ought to try and make the best of it. "Did I tell you Dr. Barbash said my vagina's like a seventeen-year-old's?" she asked, shifting her body slightly toward him.

"No, you didn't tell me that," Ed laughed. "I like your Dr. Barbash." He reached out to cuddle her and she found herself pressing against him, enjoying his warmth again. All the tension drained out of her body.

She stared down at the blanket, moved her leg a bit so the sheet fell between their bodies. Safer this way. "The tumors are also blocking my tubes. Dr. Barbash says there's no chance that I can get pregnant."

Ed jerked away from her. "You can't get pregnant?" He caught hold of himself, drew close again. Suddenly the bed was rocking. She clasped one hand tightly under the mattress to steady herself, while Ed threw the box of Ramses Extra up to the ceiling and stretched his arms out to catch it. A moment later he was on top of her, his bony knees pressing her calves, his heaviness pounding full weight on her brittle limbs. With two long-nailed fingers, he started fondling her clitoris so hard it hurt.

"Wait," she cried out. Then, softly, "I'm scared."

"I know, dear. But you won't believe how enjoyable this is going to be. You'll feel me inside you, there'll be nothing at all between our bodies. And I'll be able to stay there, even after I ejaculate." He was fondling furiously, determined to have her at the height of expectation before he entered. He tucked his cock between his legs, tightly, out of her reach until she was wet and ready.

She tried her best to pull away, but he wouldn't let go. "You don't understand," she screamed in exasperation. Then: "I'm scared you'll leave me."

"Why would I leave you?" His grip loosened slightly as he paused to formulate that question. In that brief moment she was able to work her body loose.

"Well, Dr. Barbash isn't certain, but I *might* also have a wart virus. If so, then I'd more than likely infect you." She crossed her legs. Tighter. "It would be stupid to take chances."

His face hardened. His eyes glazed over. He'd gotten VD once, years ago, when he'd first graduated college. It was no big thing, he went to a clinic and got a series of shots—but those doctors insisted on lecturing him about what venereal disease could do to the body—diabetes, blindness. "I had a checkup last month and the doctor didn't find anything suspicious," he said, half to himself.

"I know. But women usually develop symptoms first." She took his cock in her hands, fondling slowly, silently trying to see if she could feel warts, lumps, pimples, scabs. She couldn't. "My mother could have taken DES without being aware of it," she continued. "DES babies often display the same cell changes one finds in a wart virus."

"I had a blister on my finger a few weeks ago," he said. "Maybe that's what spread the infection."

"I don't think the warts were from your finger. It's probably my fault, not yours."

"It's nobody's *fault,* dear. We were only being human. We were only loving each other." He took her in his arms again.

Yes, she repeated to herself, we were only loving each other. Her body relaxed. His arms made her feel secure and protected. Even at a time like this, he seemed more concerned for her than for himself, as if placing the other person first was what love meant to him. For her it was more complicated—she'd had to work hard not to reject Ed, the way she'd rejected her parents' love. If only she'd realized it would be so hard to draw away again, she would have been more cautious. When she thought of all the times she'd harmlessly pressed Leroy against her to satisfy some need. It somehow never dawned on her that Ed would have needs of his own. And so many needs. "I don't know what to do," she said through her tears. "I only know I love you. I love you so much."

"Love you back." He said the words abstractly, letting his body slide away from her. The two of them lay side by side, on their backs. Jana thought about how someday, maybe in twenty years, they'd have separate beds, like his parents did. If only it could be as simple as that. If only he never had to touch her again. If only she didn't find herself wanting him.

She felt the need to keep talking, the way she used to take his cock (or she called it *penis* back then) in her hands so she'd be certain of where it was. She needed to keep him awake beside her. "I guess it's up to you whether or not you want to risk sleeping unprotected," she said.

Risk. Echoing in his ears, the word itself frightened him more than the sense of risk. To hear Jana use that word. "Life is a risk," he answered, perhaps aloud.

"I'm sorry, sweetheart." Jana petted the back of his hand. Long, clean strokes, one direction only. The motion soothed both of them. A few minutes ago there had been so much to say, but the words wouldn't come now. They would have to talk more about it, she supposed, then they'd decide together. With luck maybe it would take a week or two. She felt so tired.

Ed reached out to draw her onto his shoulder, maybe hold her until she drifted off to sleep. But his arm froze in midair. They'd come so close, another minute and he'd have been inside her. He wanted to pound the bed, strike out at something. Anything.

Quickly he was on top of her, large, enormous, catching her off-guard. Her legs spread wider than ever, he was inside her before either of them could think twice. He was naked, full, inside her with passion, loving her, proving she was worth the risk, and always would be. Proving to himself how much he was able to love her.

Jana's mouth fell open. Instinctively her arms closed tight around his back. "That was dumb," she laughed. She felt alive, awake again. She wanted to keep him next to her forever. She wanted to keep him *inside* her forever. She felt his sperm trickling warmly down her leg. "That was dumb," she said again. What a dumb, wonderful way to begin the holiday season.

CHAPTER TEN

Mix Grenadine and Seltzer

"I THOUGHT executives had secretaries to do their Christmas shopping," Jana teased as she and Ed headed down Lexington Avenue toward Gimbel's.

"Sounds to me like your vision of executives comes from the those Hollywood comedies they made in the forties and fifties," Ed laughed.

"I'll make it clear from the start: I am *not* buying gifts for your mistress. Besides, if I recall those movies correctly, the lacy black nightgown always ends up in the box he gives his wife, and the perfume is a fragrance his wife's allergic to."

"Right. I'm amazed your parents let you see such movies. They could have ruined your character."

"They did, they did," she laughed.

"You can say that again." Ed pulled her close and playfully felt her up through her down jacket. "We've been seeing each other for almost three months. Haven't you learned more from me than from those movies?"

"Sure, but it doesn't hurt to remind you," Jana teased.

"Seriously, though," Ed said, "shopping for Christmas has always been a high point of my year. Even growing up, I loved Christmas—not only getting things, but trying to pick out the right gifts for people I cared about. I always felt shortchanged by those aunts and uncles who wrote out a check and told me to buy what I wanted."

"If you feel that way, why did you ask me to come along tonight? I've never met your sister and her kids. How am I going to help you select presents for them?"

"I trust your taste." Ed pushed her before him in the revolving door.

"You don't know my taste."

"Sure I do. Look at that hat you're wearing. Now *that's* taste. Wherever did you find it?"

"Oh, I have my places," Jana said, stopping herself before admitting she bought it at the Canal Street flea market. She'd learned early on that Ed had a distaste for anything purchased secondhand. Her hat was unusual, to be sure, a tapestry cap with flaps over the ears and fur trim. Ed probably assumed she'd bought it in some Madison Avenue or Soho boutique. Surely he would know that such things couldn't be purchased at Gimbel's. It had been years since she'd been in a department store, and never during the Christmas rush.

"If I were smart, I'd probably be keeping one eye out for something for Ed while we're in Gimbel's," she told herself, at the same time questioning if she'd have enough energy to come back here. She'd been wondering for weeks what to get him. Records seemed a natural choice, but his taste in music was too esoteric to pinpoint. She knew he loved Sarah Vaughan, for example, but might look askance at an album recorded in 1956 because the albums she cut in 1953 or 1958 were far better. When they were in Tower Records last week he found a John Coltrane album he wanted, then double-checked it and realized he wasn't playing with quite the right people, so put it back in the bin. There was always clothing, but she'd never shopped for a man before. The jackets and shirts that caught her eye in windows were the Italian cuts, and let's face it, Ed had a conventional body.

Losing patience with the men, women, and children roving through the aisles, she began pushing people aside to make a path for herself. Ed mumbled apologies as he followed in her wake. "This crowd's nothing compared to what it will be three weeks from now. That's why I suggested we get started right after Thanksgiving," he told her. "I sometimes like the excitement of all the people shopping at the last minute, though—that's part of the holiday festivities." Ed wandered over to a table of Hummel music boxes. "My eleven-year-old niece might love these," he said. "What do you think?"

"I think they're tacky and exactly what she could buy in a department store in Indiana, or anywhere else in the country. Why don't you get something distinctly 'New York'? We could probably find great music boxes at the WBAI craft fair."

"I know, but children—or at least my sister's kids—don't want to be different. They expect exactly what everyone else has."

"That's what used to drive me crazy about the kids I grew up with. You don't think you ought to try to improve her taste?"

"There's not much I can do about it, is there? I see my sister and her kids maybe once every two years. It's especially hard now that they're getting to be teenagers, but I try to buy gifts that fit their life-style."

Jana was speechless. The ground floor of Gimbel's at the start of the Christmas season was definitely not the place for earth-shattering insights, but she couldn't help remembering how, when she'd first left home, she'd bought a few birthday or Chanukah gifts for her parents. She finally gave up when she realized they were never used—the vase sat on the top shelf of a kitchen cabinet, the unique stone candle holders were shoved in a drawer. Her selection of gifts, even gift-giving itself, had been a defensive statement that she was an artist now, that she'd escaped their value system. It never crossed her mind to shop for the sort of gifts *they* might want.

Jana caught hold of herself just as Ed was selecting a glossy ceramic clown that played "Send in the Clowns." They took the elevator to the sixth floor and bought a Cuisinart for his mother. They went down to the boys department, where she actually got into the spirit of choosing a Guess sweater for his nephew, then headed for the customer service desk to get their selections wrapped.

"I've got a better idea," Jana said, looking at the line of waiting customers. "Why don't we take these home and I'll wrap them. It'll be my contribution."

"Sounds good to me." Ed didn't like the prospect of that line any better than she did. "As long as we're in the area, do you feel like a good German dinner?" he asked as they spun through the doors again.

"Great. How about the Ideal?"

"I had in mind someplace a little more relaxing. Kleine Kontatori is just down the street—you helped shop, I can spring for dinner." Much as he hated to admit it, it *did* make things easier with Jana paying her own way, but every once in a while he felt it his duty to treat her to someplace special. Kleine Kontatori might not be the most expensive restaurant in town, but it brought back memories he wanted to share with her.

He dropped some change into the bucket of a Salvation Army Santa Claus, then led her into a bakery near Second Avenue. They walked past the narrow counter, where people were lined up ordering cakes for the holidays, and up a few steps to a nearly empty dining room. "This restaurant does a huge lunch and early-evening business," Ed said, seeing her look around in dismay. "My first copy-editing job was for a small textbook house on First Avenue and 80th Street. I used to treat myself to lunch here every Friday."

"Starting the weekend in style?" Jana teased.

"More like ending the work week with a sense I'd accomplished something. Line-editing high school history books was not my forte, and the money was ridiculous. But even so, I got into the Christmas spirit—the first Christmas I had that job I spent over a month's salary on presents. Thank God for credit cards."

"At the rate you're going, you might end up spending a month's salary this year, too."

"Not much chance of that," Ed laughed. "The only way I'll overspend this year is if I buy that elephant I've had my eye on for you."

"Whatever for?" Jana asked, laughing.

"To help you lug your paintings around, of course. I thought of it the day you came back from Yaddo."

"And because of that, you're going to buy me an elephant?"

"Either an elephant or a pack mule. The elephant's cuter, though, and it's still a baby elephant. It might not grow too large."

"You just don't want to have to help me get home from the bus station."

"Did I look like I was complaining that day last summer?"

Slightly embarrassed thinking about that day, how naive she'd been, and how she'd run out of his apartment the next morning, Jana turned her attention to the five-page menu. "They have the best sauerbraten in the city," Ed commented, and when the white-haired 150-pound waitress in a ridiculous Dutch-looking blue pinafore finally arrived and took their order in a thick German accent, they both ordered sauerbraten.

Jana gazed at another waitress walking past with a drink tray. "I remember drinking Shirley Temples," she commented.

"I've never heard of them."

"Shirley Temples were devised to keep kids happy while their parents are ordering real drinks. Mix grenadine and seltzer, top it with a piece of fruit on a parasol toothpick, and the result is juvenile bliss."

"They sound horrible, but if that's what makes children happy, I promise you our children will drink them all the time."

Jana's salad fork hung in midair. "You never mentioned anything about wanting children," she said when she'd recovered enough to speak.

"I didn't say I wanted children—I thought I was getting too old. But a few little girls who resemble you running barefoot around the apartment might be sort of fun."

"Please don't say that." Jana shook her head, trying to free herself of the tension that had been building all day—first trying to get through the day at work, then Gimbel's, now this.

Ed pressed a napkin tightly against his lips. "I know Dr. Barbash said you can't get pregnant, but that would all change if those tumors were removed. I thought anyone who kept a closet full of stuffed animals must be saving them for her children."

"I collect the animals," she said flatly, without meeting his eyes.

The corners of Ed's mouth tensed. Jana could see his lips straining against cigarette-yellow teeth. Collecting stuffed animals is a hell of a lot better than Kathe and her dogs, he reminded himself. The plates arrived. Ed took two bites of food, then asked if she used the animals as models.

"No. I liked to cuddle them sometimes—before you were around," she mumbled.

"There's nothing wrong with cuddling animals. But if they're an important part of your life, I'd expect them to appear in your paintings as well."

"I can't paint to order," Jana protested, losing more patience with each word. She recalled those first meetings with APL, when Ed suggested she work on drawings to include in the exhibition. "I don't choose my subjects, they choose me. And I'm working hard to get my work less figurative. When I *do* work with the figure, I concentrate on muscle tension. Stuffed, flaccid bodies offer no resistance—you can form stuffed animals into any shape you want, make them fit your body, that's why children love them. Translate that into painting, and it would be like working with watercolors."

"What about the rigid bodies on Steiff animals?"

"Ed, please, I know what I'm doing." Ed was as bad as Harriman, trying to force her into working with oil. Harriman, at least, based his arguments on experience. Were she having this conversation with Marilyn or Gary, they'd get into a discussion about foreshortening and developing tension in the figure—talking with other artists helped her work out the process, even if they didn't have any answers. But Ed wasn't familiar with artistic terminology, and explaining things to him wasn't worth the effort.

No, it wasn't a question of effort. Being with Ed still felt strange to her. She was accustomed to hiding behind her art, talking about technique to avoid more personal subjects, especially with men. Avoidance, tonight, was bordering on calamity. Ed's face was as red as that Santa Claus.

She ran her eyes over the Christmas presents piled up on the chair next to him, recalling one present she'd gotten as a child—a painting of Lady and the Tramp. The only uncle who'd encouraged her art, a butcher cum Sunday painter, painted that for her eighth birthday. He set the two gold dogs on a dark red background, painted white borders to save her parents the expense of a frame. She'd tacked it on her wall with a nail, and never again felt close to him. Five years later, when she was painting more seriously than he was, he gave her his stamp collection. Neither gift was appropriate, but at least he'd tried, which was more than her other aunts and uncles had done. She had the frightening vision of Ed trying too, spending $100 on a Steiff animal to give her for Christmas. Assuming we're still together this Christmas, she thought, remembering that tomorrow was the board meeting scheduled to discuss Matt Fillmore's drawing.

"Getting back to the subject," she said calmly, almost as if she were making peace with her uncle, "I used to think about adopting a child, but I'd never want the responsibility of creating life."

"As I said, a family isn't my main objective. If that's how you feel about children, then I promise never to bring up the subject again." Ed signaled for the check and a refill on coffee. His gaze wandered the room as he found himself thinking about how, with Kathe, there was always her craziness to use as a cover. Half the time, Kathe wasn't even aware of what he was doing or saying; she just wanted someone there to support her. His conversations with Kathe never got out of hand, as this one had. "Maybe it's just hypertension," he thought, glancing up at Jana waiting impatiently for him to finish eating.

℘ ℘

On the way home, Jana insisted they stop at the discount drug store on Broadway and pick up some wrapping paper. Yet when they got to the apartment, instead of opening the new paper, she went into the kitchen and came back with a roll of Reynolds Wrap. Ed turned on the television and watched silently while Jana sat cross-legged on the floor, folding the corners of the foil carefully around the box holding the ceramic clown. He wanted to stop her, to remind her that his niece was important to him, that as long as she'd bought the wrapping paper she ought to use it. But something in Jana's movements, the energy with which she set to wrapping, warned him not to speak.

Aware of his eyes on her, she selected a sheet of wrapping paper, spread it on the floor, and set the foil-covered box in the center of it. She double-folded a piece of tape and stuck the center of the box securely to the paper, then folded the paper around the rest loosely. She pinned a bow in the center of the top, then asked to borrow his penknife.

She pulled out a small blade and began making quick, narrow slits in the wrapping paper, along all four sides. She unpinned the top bow, fluffed out the sides, and pinned the bow again, then sprayed the whole thing with hairspray until the paper became stiff. Finally she held it up for his examination.

Ed stared in wonderment. It looked like a Chinese lantern. The sides ballooned out, and the silver paper glittered between the slits. "It's fabulous!" he said.

"You'll have to be careful shipping it. These sides will crush easily."

"More than worth the effort. That wrapping looks like a present in itself."

"It's based on the same concept as those string decorations we used to make in arts and crafts. The ones where you blew up a balloon, pasted different colored wool around it, then popped the balloon."

"I remember those. They never looked that great, though. Leave it to an artist to be creative," he teased.

"Resourceful, not creative," Jana said. "It comes from wanting to give presents and being broke. The first few years I was living in the city, I didn't have a steady job and couldn't even get a charge card. I remember one year I took a lot of my old sketches and watercolors, practice pieces. I cut them up and sewed them into handmade books, then gave them to friends as Christmas presents."

"I wish I'd known you then," Ed mused. "I'll bet they were something else."

"Be nice, and maybe I'll make you one this year." Jana smiled up at him, then devoted all her attention to his sister's jewelbox, trying to decide how it might be wrapped.

Ed could have spent the rest of the evening entranced by her movements. Was this the same woman who, two hours ago, had gotten hysterical over the mere mention of children? Jana's ability to bounce back from her little episodes was as much a marvel as her creatively wrapped presents were. He might envy his friends in relationships with calm, secure women, but that very stability would more than likely put him off. His mother's outbursts had set a pattern he all but expected in women. And hysterical or not, Jana's self-assurance was clear to him; the more she fought against admitting it the clearer it became. He could be supportive and responsive to her moods, but he didn't have to carry the world's weight on his shoulders.

CHAPTER ELEVEN

Not Your Decision or Mine

THE MEETING had been called for two o'clock, but people began drift-
ing in fifteen minutes early. Pretending to busy herself with last-minute
arrangements, Jana watched out of a corner of her eye while Natalie
chatted away. They'd attempted, in choosing their board, to achieve a
balance of arts supporters and business expertise, but this would be the
first time their values were put to a test.

Jana and Natalie had been over this a hundred times in the past two
weeks. Jana took a steadfast position: we invited an artist whose work we
respect; he submitted pieces which are entirely appropriate to the theme
of the exhibition. Yes, *Power and Light* raises issues the exhibition's
sponsor would prefer to avoid; it's also an extremely strong work. We
cannot, under any circumstances, ask Matt Fillmore to substitute another piece. And Natalie's position was: that's not your decision or
mine. The board will decide. She might hope they'd agree with Jana, but
she wasn't about to tell them what to do.

Much as she hated to admit it, Jana knew Natalie was right: they
couldn't act without their board. More importantly, they needed the
board's corporate jockeying for position if they were going to have a leg
to stand on with APL.

And where did she stand with Ed? All of the sudden there was more
than her job, more than one exhibition, more than art-world prestige at
stake. If they could get the board behind them, then even if worst came
to worst and APL refused to permit that work in the show, they could
conceivably come up with last-minute backing. The exhibition might

not be on as grand a scale, but that would only make it closer to their original proposal. Even if APL retained sponsorship, Jana was beginning to wonder if her relationship with Ed could stand the strain. If there *was* strain; for all she knew, APL's board might readily agree to show the work. Don't count your chickens before they hatch, she reminded herself, glancing up as the final two board members walked in. But also: don't put all your eggs in one basket.

Natalie passed out prints of all six slides Matt Fillmore had sent them, checked to make sure everyone had received copies of the articles Jana gathered, then turned the meeting over to their board president.

"I think it's fairly obvious from reading these articles, and the passages Jana has highlighted, what position our curator takes," Bill began. "And I'll be the first to concede that the articles are extremely articulate at addressing the dangers involved in corporate censorship. But what's the other side of the coin?"

"The Paperworks Space loses its credibility," Jana said. "We could get all the sponsorship in the world, but if we can't convince the artists we respect to show with us, what good does it do?"

"I was thinking more of our sponsor's predicament," Bill said with a good-natured chuckle.

"APL has gotten off easy so far with this new generating plant," another board member began. "There was a bit of negative publicity when they were first granted the land, but even at the time the incident was overshadowed by the government's takeover of reservation land in the Allegheny Mountains so they could build the Kinzua Dam. If APL leaves the work in the show, some people will notice, but it will also go over the heads of many viewers. If they attempt to censor the work, they're risking an onset of negative publicity once again—not only for censorship, but for the generating plant itself."

"In other words, our job would be to convince them they don't want that publicity?" someone asked.

"And to convince them The Paperworks Space has the power to start such publicity in motion," Natalie added somewhat doubtfully.

"Don't forget, we're not dealing with a show at the gallery here, but with a city-wide exhibition," Gary pointed out. "We might be in a much stronger position than you realize."

"There's another aspect to all this," Jana said. She pulled a few pages out of her folder and passed copies around. "This is an excerpt from our original proposal to APL. Most of you have seen it before. It's the section discussing the work of artists we're intending to include in the exhibition. I recall writing those descriptions, and how careful I was to allay APL's fears that the works might be controversial." She recalled that day when Ed had driven her down to the gallery, how she'd watched him looking closely at Lou Daniels' drawings, and silently imagined him putting any fears of controversy to rest once and for all. "To get to the point," she continued, pushing such thoughts aside, "it wasn't until APL insisted upon more prestigious artists that we came up with Matt Fillmore."

"Whew," someone exclaimed. "You're really trying to pass the buck, aren't you?" Another board member pointed out that there were any number of prestigious artists around, and it had still been a decision of The Paperworks Space to include Matt Fillmore.

Bill sat quietly, taking it all in. "Your point is well made, Jana," he said after a ten-minute discussion. "I'd say that, if worst came to worst, we might remind APL of their insistence on name artists, but the purpose would be to emphasize Matt Fillmore's prestige. Frankly, I'd prefer to find other ways of convincing them to leave the work in the exhibition."

"Assuming that 'leaving the work in the exhibition' is our ultimate objective," another board member said. "It seems to me that hasn't been decided yet. Among other things, this piece doesn't accurately depict Indian life. I did a little research also, and discovered that no Indians in New York State, or anywhere in the Northeast, ever lived in teepees. It was far too cold. So, if we wanted to ask that the work be withdrawn, we would have an aesthetic basis as well."

"We're talking about art, not history," Jana said, fighting to keep her voice level.

"I don't think there's any question that the teepee image immediately identifies Native American life to the general public," Natalie cut in before Jana said something they'd all regret.

"Okay," Bill said. "I think the first order of business is to make up our minds: do we stick to our guns about including this drawing or is the matter up for discussion and possible compromise?"

Jana noticeably tensed as board members began discussing the pros and cons. Gary, Larry Rivers, and luckily, Bill Fitch all strongly supported her position that the work had to stay. She found herself wondering what position Ed would take. At least no one was suggesting she get him involved. She had feared the worst, had pictured Natalie rattling off all the little extras Ed had done for them last spring when he'd first been interested in her. And when she refused to speak to him, Natalie would comment that she didn't care enough about what happened at The Paperworks Space, the relationship was the only thing that seemed to matter. The whole board would end up attacking her for not caring enough about her job.

"Oh Christ," Jana told herself. "Here I go on another one of my guilt trips." She was feeling guilty that she had the show at Walker to prepare for, that she couldn't devote her full attention to the crisis at hand. But instead of getting upset with her perfectionist goals, she was finding fault with Natalie, with the board, with the relationship. "It's a wonder Ed puts up with me," she mused. "I can barely tolerate myself at a time like this."

At "a time like this" her attention should be focused on the discussion. She might not want to hear what they were saying, but she had no choice. Two board members, in particular, seemed adamant that the name of the game was compromise, but the arguments Bill and Larry Rivers presented finally won out, and everyone on the board was brought around to a decision that the drawing had to remain at all costs.

"Next order of business: how do we proceed from here?" Bill asked.

"You're the board president," Natalie said. "I would hope that APL would be attentive to your opinions concerning the work."

"Didn't you say you were instrumental in Matt Fillmore's Dallas commission?" Jana asked, already knowing the answer. "It would seem that you could approach Frank Markowitz as one CEO to another, as someone who took similar risks with your own company."

"Certainly I can attempt that, but the controversial aspects of Matt's work never came to the forefront of that Nationbank commission."

"Pure luck," someone mumbled, to which Bill responded that he'd been just thinking the same thing. The group broke out in much-needed laughter. After they calmed down, Bill began making a list of the aspects he wanted to stress to APL: the need to avoid negative publicity about that generating plant was first on the list, but what else?

"Free speech in general," someone suggested.

"The fact that the message will go over the heads of many viewers."

"Don't forget, there are six exhibition sites; this drawing will be at Lincoln Center. A lot of viewers will only see one or two of the sites and will perceive APL's original message—'look at the efforts we're making on behalf of your city'—without any knowledge that one artist saw fit to argue with their 'good intentions.' Unless, of course, the higher-ups at APL want to draw people's attention to the controversy."

"The drawing will still be in the catalog. Weren't we relying upon that catalog to provide wider coverage than the six sites?"

"If need be, I could probably ensure that the catalog is not distributed as widely as we'd planned," Natalie began.

"We'll cross that bridge when we come to it," Bill said. "Far be it from me to put any ideas into APL's head."

"As I said in my letter that accompanied the articles about similar incidents, I think it's wise to point out we're not trying to pull a fast one," Jana said. "APL will have copies of this drawing in their hands in plenty of time to seek the advice of their own board and make a calm decision. We could have held out longer if we'd wanted to. But the fact that we're confronting them with the problem almost as soon as it comes to our attention should speak well for the gallery's professionalism and social responsibility."

Bill checked over his list again. "I'd say this gives us a pretty good beginning," he said. "But I've got my work cut out for me. I'll give Frank Markowitz a call tomorrow morning and try to arrange a meeting."

"Let us know what happens," Natalie said.

"That should be the least of your worries."

✿ ✿

Bill called the next morning to say he was having lunch with Frank on Thursday. "Just one more night," Jana thought. She wanted to make every moment left with Ed count. And then, on Thursday, she found herself counting: five more hours until seven o'clock, four more hours, three more hours . . . They'd arranged to meet in one of their favorite restaurants. All afternoon she was hoping Bill would call to let them know how the meeting went, but no such luck. As Natalie reminded her, it was nice enough that Bill was taking time out from his job on the gallery's behalf for the second time this week. They couldn't make more demands on him.

Jana pushed the wild mushroom ravioli around on her plate. A house specialty, this was one of her favorite dishes, but tonight it seemed tasteless. Ed twirled two strands of angel hair pasta on his fork, letting the peas and baby shrimp fall in the process. Didn't Jana realize he knew? He felt it would be best to wait for her to bring up the subject, but he couldn't wait forever. They continued eating in silence, until Ed couldn't stand it any longer. "Bill Fitch spoke with Frank this afternoon," he said, making no effort whatsoever to hide his anger. "I wish you'd told me." He turned his face away.

"That wouldn't have done any good."

"It might not have done *you* any good, you mean. All you were thinking about was yourself. Not about me, not about my job."

"I didn't want to mix business with pleasure. It would just confuse things. Besides, it wasn't as if we were keeping it secret forever. I knew Bill would talk to Frank."

"Dammit, Jana, it's not Frank's job to find out about such things, it's *mine*. Frank expects me to keep track of the exhibition's progress and let him know the minute there are problems that can't be easily solved. Especially in this case, Frank found it hard to believe I didn't already know. He raked me over the coals for having held out on him."

Jana sat there stunned, batting back tears. "I'm sorry," she said. "It never dawned on me that not telling you could cause more problems." They stared at each other, trying to see who'd break down first. "What happens now?" Jana asked.

"With the exhibition or with my job?" Ed asked accusingly. Or with us, Jana wanted to add. Biting her bottom lip, she waited for him to continue. "Frank's going to have to speak with the board of directors." Ed's tone softened just a little.

See there, Jana wanted to point out, Frank can't act without his board. Well, it's the same thing at The Paperworks Space. My job might not be as high-paying as yours is, but it matters a lot to me, too. I couldn't tell you about it before I had the board's approval, any more than Frank can act without the board's approval now. But what was the use of getting caught on such a merry-go-round? That wasn't what this conversation was about; that wasn't what she read in Ed's anger. She sat there sucking her breath in.

"I can't be much help to you when I don't know what's going on," Ed said.

Jana drew back. "I don't want that kind of help."

"You don't know what kind of help; *I* don't know what kind of help!"

He's screaming out of frustration with himself, not out of anger at me, Jana realized.

"Look, it's my job to help The Paperworks Space organize the exhibition," Ed continued. "Frank knows we're seeing each other, and I'm sure he realizes we discuss the exhibition. As he reminded me again today, I've been working at APL long enough to know where the professional boundaries are drawn. But you've got to be willing to confide in me. Otherwise our relationship won't be based on trust, either."

"Trust me—that's what all men say," Jana laughed nervously. "You make it sound simple."

"It *is* simple." Ed sounded more confident than he felt. Working his way through college had its benefits, after all—once you'd mastered the art of selling World Books to families who couldn't pay the rent that month, you could convince people of anything. "I didn't say we could just go ahead and include that drawing, but there's not much question that we have to take some kind of action. Yours isn't the first program we've funded that's become more controversial than we'd anticipated. The use and misuse of energy is a hot issue these days."

Not wanting to add to *that* debate, Jana changed the subject. "Frank's not thinking of taking you off the exhibition, is he?"

"The thought probably crossed his mind. But I've invested too much in this project already, and Marsha's got her hands full with other proposals," Ed said, reassuring himself at the same time. "As I said, Frank knows we're seeing each other. If he was planning to replace me, he'd have done that months ago." Ed tapped one finger firmly against his palm. "Like it or not, you're stuck with me."

"I'm liking it more and more." Jana tried to smile. Ed hadn't told her what he thought of that drawing, she realized. Surely he'd seen it by now. The last thing she'd expected was that they'd be able to avoid a political discussion tonight.

Ed placed his hand over hers. "I know it's been hectic for you. It's been hectic for both of us," he said. "After the exhibition opens in May, maybe I'll take some time off and we'll go on a vacation, just the two of us. How does a cruise to Nassau sound?"

"We'll see," she said. It sounded boring as hell: costume parties on shipboard, food and more food, gambling once you got to port, shopping for painted shells with a hundred fat grandmothers in sleeveless dresses who'd put on too much perfume. Didn't Ed understand yet that she was happiest when she was working, that she wanted *more* time to paint, not less? Sometimes she felt as if she'd been living a lie all these months, wining and dining at restaurants Ed could afford more easily than she could, playing the same games with her lover that she was forced to play with society matrons. She couldn't even cling to him and forget everything else these days. Natalie once commented that she worked better when there was a man in her life; knowing the evening was planned, she got more accomplished during the day. Jana thought she'd enjoy having her life structured around a relationship, especially since she'd been finding it increasingly difficult to spend twenty-four hours a day painting. Instead she felt as if everything she'd been struggling so hard for was slipping away from her.

"Four months from now the exhibition will be open and your show in Minneapolis will be over; you'll finally be able to relax," Ed continued.

"No, I won't. Even if everything goes well, it will only prove I can reach further, get a bigger show of my own work, curate a larger exhibition."

"I don't know how much larger you can expect," Ed laughed.

Jana was, as usual, humorless. "If I don't *expect*, then what's the use? I'm really sorry, Ed, but I can't sit back and watch other people get ahead of me. We're not talking about climbing some corporate ladder, we're talking about my *life.*"

"I'm aware of that," Ed said, trying to repress his irritation; using her painter's mask for protection was one thing, but when she set herself above the corporate world it couldn't help but grate on him. "It still doesn't make any sense to get all caught up with the next project or the project after that," he continued. "You have to give yourself over to what's needed at the moment, and do the best job you possibly can. That's part of being a good executive."

"I'm a perfectly good executive or curator or whatever," Jana mumbled into her dirty plate. Those words slipped out before she could stop herself—words she said by rote now. They were almost as easy as saying "I love you," and equally meaningless at the moment. She used to be good. Everything she did, she did well. Until now, that is. "You're an incredible lover," she remembered Ed whispering last fall when she was still a virgin; the words sounded like a taunt now.

"Don't mind me," she said, catching hold of herself again. "I build up adrenalin by going in circles, but I always come through it and get things done in the end. I'm not used to having someone around watching, that's all."

"Having someone around is new to me, too."

Jana tried to smile. "Any idea how long till it becomes comfortable?"

"Nope. That's what keeps life interesting. When couples get too comfortable, they start taking each other for granted."

"I guess."

"You don't sound very convinced."

"I don't know. Being on strange ground is time-consuming. I don't seem to have either the time or the energy to accomplish things. I'll be lucky if we make it through this exhibition, let alone a larger one."

"You'll make it through the exhibition, believe me. But even if there are more hitches between now and the opening, you don't have to blame yourself for them. Problems crop up all the time; you needn't take them so personally."

"Okay, I take things too personally, but that's the way I am," Jana admitted defensively.

"You don't really see yourself. Take this drawing, for instance. I know, you thought I was attacking you, but I wasn't, I was attacking your not telling me. There's a difference. I might have been angry, but that doesn't mean I don't love you."

The distinction was harder for her to accept. "I feel as if I haven't been on top of things lately," she said. "Ever since we've been together, it's almost as if I haven't been paying attention to anything else. Sometimes I worry that we won't have anything more to talk about once the exhibition's over, that we'll get bored with each other." She recalled her astonishment last summer: here was someone praising her when she wasn't standing on her head to get attention. Six or seven months ago, she'd been able to enjoy that praise, but the more often she heard it the less it seemed to fit. All they had to do was start talking about the exhibition for a minute, and she had the perfect excuse to discredit all their tender moments. If she'd had to work harder for Ed's love, maybe it would be easier to trust it.

"Don't mistake fatigue for boredom," Ed said. They sat in silence, casting careful glances at each other, as if checking each other over again, rethinking their involvement. He knew Jana's modus operandi by now: if she was worried about something concerning the gallery, she could talk to him about frustrations in her painting. If she was struggling with things in her painting, either she complained about the gallery or shut him out completely. He tried to be patient and understanding, he tried not to push her either sexually or emotionally, he felt as if he understood her struggle to come to grips with that traumatic summer twenty-five years ago. But he also longed for the day when she'd be open and honest with him. Everything in due time, he assured himself. "You're stuck with me," he told her.

CHAPTER TWELVE

Free Speech

FRANK MET with APL's board of directors; Frank, Ed, and Marsha met with Jana, Natalie, and Bill Fitch; the holidays intervened; Frank met with Bill; Ed met with Natalie and Jana; Jana ran back to her apartment for a few hours after work to have some time to paint; Frank and Ed passed each other in the halls; Jana and Natalie met with Phyllis to discuss the promotion campaign; Frank suggested he'd like to talk with Matt Fillmore; The Paperworks Space board met; Ed and Jana found other things to talk about over dinner; Bill told Frank he felt it would be best if the administrations resolved this issue without involving the artist; Jana and Natalie met with Phyllis to continue plans for the gala; Jana spoke with Matt Fillmore twice and carefully avoided any mention of his slides; Jana, Natalie, and Bill met with Ed; Frank met with the board of directors; negotiations dragged on until the middle of February. Then, just after Presidents' Day, Frank called to arrange a meeting with Natalie, Jana, and Bill. "Off the record," Bill told Natalie he was reasonably certain APL had accepted the work's inclusion; "off the record," Ed told Jana he loved her.

Jana walked into APL's conference room. So much had happened since the first time she'd entered these offices last spring that she no longer felt uncomfortable in such lush surroundings. "Let's just hope that, after today, I'll be welcome back," she thought. Ed was, as usual, late for the meeting.

"Before we get down to technicalities, I want to reiterate the fact that, despite the conflicts which have arisen, APL's commitment to the Artistic Response to the Environment exhibition remains as solid as it was at the onset of the project," Frank began.

Jana cast a slight smile in Natalie's direction, then in Ed's. Ed had his nose pointed at the heavy oak table. "If Bill doesn't know Ed and I are seeing each other, he's certainly not going to suspect it from *this* meeting," Jana thought.

"As you probably suspected, our board decided that, in the interest of free speech, Matt Fillmore's *Power and Light* drawing (he winced when he mentioned the title) should be included in the exhibition. We do, however, insist upon one stipulation. We see it as imperative that APL make its own position known as well." He nodded to Ed, whose fingers were nervously drumming on a manila envelope in front of him.

"We've drawn up a statement presenting our views," Ed began. "And we'd like it presented alongside the drawing—on a plaque at the exhibition, as well as in the catalog." He opened the envelope and passed copies of the statement around:

> The Indians who lived on the Onondaga Reservation were relocated by the federal government in 1974. At that time, the prospect of Associated Power and Light building a generating plant on that land was not even under discussion. By the time the land was granted to APL in May of 1981, those who had been driven from their homes had successfully adjusted to lives elsewhere. We could not have given the land back to the Seneca Nation even had we wished to.
>
> Work on APL's new generating plant is scheduled to begin in the summer of 1986. The additional power we will provide upon its completion will help enrich the lives of all New Yorkers.

"Free speech means free speech for everyone," Frank said.

Bill glanced from Natalie to Jana and back again. Drawing a blank on both faces, he saw it as his duty to respond. "It might be best if we discuss this with members of The Paperworks Space board. Hopefully, we can get back to you by the end of the week."

"We'll also have to talk with the artist," Jana said.

"Of course, I understand perfectly," Frank said, rising. The meeting had been adjourned.

"Whew," Jana exclaimed as they walked out the revolving doors to the street.

"I have a little time before I'm due back at the office. Why don't we get some coffee?" Bill suggested. His "have to talk to members of the board" was, as Jana and Natalie realized, an excuse; obviously, *they* were the ones he wanted to talk with. They headed for that same coffee shop where Jana and Natalie had bumped into Ed ten months ago.

"I'd venture to say we got off lucky," Bill said as they sat down. "We realized that, even at best, we might have to make slight compromises, and this one's about as harmless as they come."

"Tell that to Matt Fillmore," Jana responded.

"I will, if you want me to," Bill offered, gracious as usual.

Feeling Natalie glaring at her, Jana shook the knots from her neck and apologized. "I didn't mean to be so glib about it, I'm just not looking forward to Matt's reaction. Thanks for your offer, but I'm the curator, it's my job to tell him."

"We can both tell him, if you want. I've worked with him on other projects, and I know him socially, so I might be a little better at presenting the corporate view."

"You'll be a *lot* better at presenting the corporate view," Jana laughed.

Bill agreed to call Matt and set up a meeting as soon as he could. "Also, remember something—the very fact that Matt's willing to have his work included in this exhibition to begin with suggests that, even though he might be critical of APL's actions, he's willing to enter into a dialogue."

"I'll keep than in mind when we talk to him," Jana promised. Leave it to Bill to be rational.

ↄ ↄ

Friday's luncheon meeting was supposed to include Natalie, but some last minute problems came up that Natalie had to attend to, so Jana was left on her own to meet with Bill and Matt. She'd been introduced to Matt at a few openings, but the only times they'd talked had been on the phone since they'd started working on the exhibition. "He's always seemed pleasant enough," she told herself as she headed for the restaurant. Even after six years working as a curator, she was still a bit in awe of big-name artists whose work she respected.

She also hadn't remembered how tall Matt was—over six feet, with a very firm handshake. Nervously, she sat down. Thankfully, Bill and Matt had a lot to say to each other, and Bill was as adept as ever at conversation. Drawing Jana in, they chatted about reasonably safe topics such as Reagan's recent cutbacks in Medicare and support for the arts. "Art's been running into more and more problems of late," Jana said, sensing her opening.

The lead-in was stronger than she'd anticipated. Conversation halted, and she felt Matt's intense eyes staring her down. "Such as?" he asked.

"Such as APL wasn't exactly delighted with your *Power and Light* piece."

Matt gave a slight laugh. "I wasn't exactly intending to delight them. I did that work especially for the exhibition."

"I figured as much. It's an extremely strong piece," Jana hastened to add.

"But they want it out of the show, right? Well, no way. Take that out, you can take *all* my work out."

"As a matter of fact, we've convinced them that censorship wouldn't be in anyone's best interests, including theirs," Bill said, not batting an eyelash.

"I'm still hearing a *but* at the end of that sentence."

"Free speech means free speech for everyone, including Big Business," Jana said, echoing Frank's words. "APL wants to be certain viewers are also presented with their point of view." She passed Matt the envelope. "In the catalog, and on a plaque at the exhibition," she added while he was reading it.

"Sort of lessens the effect, don't you think?" he asked sarcastically.

"Not really. If anything, giving their point of view might even heighten the controversy, draw more attention to your work."

"To my work, or to the political statement?"

"Why did you do the drawing in the first place if it wasn't to make the statement?" Jana asked.

"Touché," Matt said dryly. Then he suggested he might want to add his own statement.

"That drawing seems statement enough, and its power comes from letting viewers make up their own minds," Jana said. Natalie might have come up with a comment such as "art enlightens, it doesn't preach," but Jana had never been forced to sit through the art history and art appreciation courses that Natalie and most other people had suffered in their younger days.

"Besides, the eye absorbs quicker than the mind," Bill added. "Many people will respond to the image and pay no attention whatever to the text."

Matt asked for a few days to think it over.

"We promised APL we'd get back to them by the end of the week, and Jana also has to get working on the catalog copy," Bill said. "Actually, we've been in negotiations concerning your drawing since before the holidays. Everyone was hoping we'd win unconditional acceptance, which is why we didn't tell you about it before."

Matt let his eyes rest between his two companions. Then he read the statement again. "Do you fight this hard for all your artists?" he asked, casting an almost sheepish smile in Jana's direction. He wasn't giving in, he wasn't saying the words *Yes, I'll remain in the show,* but he'd obviously intended that smile to speak for him.

"Only the artists I think are worth it," Jana laughed, taking a bite of food for the first time in the past fifteen minutes. She was almost beginning to enjoy this expensive lunch.

℘ ℘

With the major task of the past three months successfully accomplished, Jana could finally devote her attention to preparing for the show at the Walker. Ten days later, already March and starting to get warm outside, she stood in the center of her studio, giving the "city life" paintings one last look before crating them. The last time these paintings had been spread out before her eyes was in August, when they were photographed for slides submitted to DCA. Jana counted on her fingers: September, October, November, December, January, February, March—seven months. It felt more like seven years. The shadow of the dead body in the corner of *Mulberry Street* could be easily mistaken for a photographic reproduction, yet she distinctly recalled thinking at the time it had broken new ground.

Three years ago, when she'd begun work on these paintings, she and Gary had long talks about photo-realism. Gary had pointed out the individuality of her focus: "If ten artists paint the same street at the same time of day, they'll all focus on something different. Your talent lies in your ability to pick out the inconsequential fragment that no one else pays attention to." And Jana had chalked up those "inconsequential fragments" to the hours on end that she had spent walking around the city with a camera, using the lens as a tool for keeping the object close yet distant. She'd described the snapshots tacked on her easel as a device for making the transformative process easier.

"Transformed into what?" she asked herself now. Transformation couldn't be summoned, it happened when she wasn't looking, and it stemmed from an inward focus, not an outward one. Its roots were in abstraction, even when the final image was immediately recognizable. She recalled the process of painting that first successful self-portrait last August. She'd begun by drawing a bathing cap for the skull, put a smudge on her cheek, and ended by painting heavy, crisscrossed lines weighing the mind down. The original attempt to capture her inner beauty had provided, instead, a portrait of the mind *blocking* radiance. And she'd gone on from there in more recent paintings, often emerging with surreal, unpredictable imagery—a hand on a shoulder appeared half-bone, half-crab claw, made more haunting by the shoulder and the arm being separated from the bodies that sustained them; a jumble of lines over a breast became recognizable as the halter top of a floral bathing suit, two flowers picked off.

The paintings spread out before her seemed stagnant by comparison, but she tried to work up the excitement again by seeing them with Gary's eye. In two weeks she'd be shipping *herself* off to Minneapolis, and if she didn't have faith in her paintings, she could hardly expect other people to appreciate them.

It was after two o'clock, and the trucker would be here at four—she'd better get moving. Once the paintings were safely packed, she could stare at the impersonal wood and pretend the crates contained her newer works. But those paintings weren't ready to show yet, either; she was still in the process of developing the new theme and the formal shifts that went along with it. Hammering the lid on the final crate, Jana wondered what Gary would say when he saw her new work. Before she realized what was happening, she found herself wondering what she'd be painting now if she'd been more in tune with her body years ago, if she and Gary had ended up as lovers.

ℝ ℝ

The crates were gone and Jana stared around a room that seemed to have doubled in size. Only then did she realize how much she'd been thinking of Gary today. What Ed would think of either the new work or the old hadn't entered her thoughts. Ever since losing her virginity, she'd felt almost estranged from this man who'd played such a huge role in her life. "My trip to Minneapolis will do us both good," she told herself. "Besides, if Ed wanted, he could go with me." She recalled her comment, last summer when they'd flirted dangerously, about how she'd sneak him into her room at Yaddo. She had to laugh at herself—she was acting as if she were the only player in this drama, as if Ed were some stuffed animal she could cram into her suitcase.

It would be no trouble to sneak Leroy into her hotel room, would it? She walked over and opened the closet door—she hadn't realized how much junk she'd been piling in here; Leroy had been pushed to the back. Mice had gotten in again, and the insulation they'd dug out of the walls was all over his mane and tail. She didn't want to touch him, let alone sleep with him.

She wondered if the cleaners would accept stuffed animals, then had second thoughts about the way they handled things: last week a blouse had been returned to her missing a shoulder pad, and over the past few months she could remember two or three melted buttons. She also couldn't bring herself to walk in and say I'd like my lion cleaned, or I'd like my *daughter's* lion cleaned. But maybe the self service places . . . She stuffed him headfirst into a shopping bag and took him to the laundromat on Third Avenue.

Her plans were for Leroy to go in the dry cleaning machine, but there was a big sign saying NO STUFFED ANIMALS, and attendants seemed to be peeking out from every crevice. Hesitantly, she looked around—the two dozen free washers all had a post or wringer in the center, Leroy would be pulled limb from limb. Finally, she spotted a double-load front-loading washer against the back wall.

She sat Leroy in the center, set it on cold water, gentle cycle, dumped in one of those double-load boxes of Tide, no bleach. She put in six quarters, pressed the button. The machine began to fill with water. Leroy sank comfortably down in it, his head bobbing just above the rising tide. Then the detergent came in; he was in a bubble bath. Now he spun slowly, head over heels. Stopped. Was he too heavy for the machine? She was about to see if she could pry the door open when he started spinning again, the other way this time, building up speed.

It was like watching a child at an amusement park. She'd spotted a popcorn machine at the front of the store, and she treated herself, like at the movies. When she got back to the machine Leroy was spinning so fast she couldn't see him. He was a yellow blur, like those sheep blurred just before she fell asleep some nights. Jana placed a piece of popcorn between her front teeth and clamped shut on it.

A half hour later all the motors and lights went off. She pulled Leroy out and set him in a laundry cart. His fur was glowing. She reached over and pulled a few pieces of stuffing out of his mane, examined his body, found two little holes, pinpricks, one on each side of his neck. She hesitated for a minute. She shouldn't take him home wet. He'd survived the washer; she supposed a little hot air wouldn't harm him.

Once he was in the dryer, she could watch him changing positions, hear his large black plastic eyes knocking against the window. His mouth kept falling open as if trying to catch hold of the pink fabric softener cloth she'd thrown in with him. When the machine stopped he ended up cradled between two side spokes, legs crossed—a pipe in his mouth would complete the picture of old-fashioned comfort.

She took him out and set him back in the shopping bag. Wait a second—on the way over he'd filled the entire bag; now he shifted loosely to one side. Could dirt have taken up that much room? She pulled his head up and watched his neck flop over the side. She pulled out one arm; it too flopped limply. He *couldn't* have lost that much stuffing. Or could he? She went back and checked the washer, reached her hand in to see if there were piles of stuffing she hadn't seen, but came up empty.

She took Leroy home, propped him up on the bed, then called Marilyn. If anyone would know about crafts and fabrics, it would be Marilyn.

"He was probably stuffed with foam," Marilyn said. "Foam dries out, especially in the heat of a dryer. That's why foam pillows have to continually be replaced. There was an advantage to those old feather pillows our grandmothers used."

Jana asked what she could do now, and Marilyn suggested she get some shredded foam from a crafts store and restuff him. "Or if you can wait a few weeks, till I'm done with this wallpaper book I'm working on, I'll help you," Marilyn offered.

Jana mentioned having to leave for Minneapolis, and working on the exhibition full time when she returned. "If I don't get it done right away, it might have to wait forever. But thanks anyway."

She ran over to a crafts store, bought two bags of foam, gold thread to stitch up his holes with, and a brown paisley ribbon to tie around his neck. She perched on the edge of the bed and held him on her lap. She took her nail scissors and enlarged the holes at his neck, stuffed two handfuls of foam in each side. No, that was too much. She took some out, sewed up the holes, then kneaded his neck to try to even out his stuffing. Next she slit a hole in the seam at the top of one arm, stuffed it with foam, sewed it up, and kneaded. She repeated the process with the other arm, then both legs. She'd used up both bags of foam, and could have used even more, but it was after six and the store would probably be closed, so she made do.

She leaned Leroy's back against the headboard, crossed his legs. Wherever she placed him, it looked as if he belonged there. He seemed delighted to be home and in his own bed again, and they'd both been through the wringer already today—she didn't have the heart to bundle him back up and whisk him off to Minneapolis.

CHAPTER THIRTEEN

Five Long Nights Alone

JANA RAISED a sleepy head from the pillow. "Oh good, you're awake," Ed said. "Are you certain you don't want me to call in late and drive you to the airport?"

"I'm positive. The last thing I need is to get stuck in traffic and miss the plane—cabbies know how to handle rush hour."

"Have it your way." Ed bent to kiss her. "Break a leg."

"Thanks." Jana moved over to his side of the bed, hoping to fall back to sleep enveloped in his leftover warmth, but she was too restless. She got up a little after eight, unpacked her suitcase to be sure she had everything she needed, then packed it again. She was taking Ed's garment bag on this trip, not her mother's suitcase—easier to keep things pressed without folding them. She put on the same gray tapestry jacket she'd worn that first day with Ed, hoping it would bring her luck. The show might be poorly reviewed, but at least Ed loved her—as she headed for the airport, that almost seemed enough.

The plane took off forty-five minutes late, but picked up time en route. Keeping her seatbelt fastened, Jana thought about Ed most of the trip. She was still thinking of Ed as she walked into the terminal and a small, heavyset woman in her early twenties accosted her. "Are you Miss Replansky?" she asked. "You look just like your photograph in our files. I'm Sharon, from Walker's internship program. Steve Whitman's busy with last-minute arrangements—he asked me to pick you up."

Stopping at the Sheraton long enough to drop off her bags, Jana noticed the daisies on the dresser. "Start with 'he loves me,'" the note said.

"I have a feeling there's always an even number of petals. All luck, all love." So Ed remembered.

Her stories of pulling apart daisies at Yaddo might have inspired the note, but Ed had been looking for an excuse to buy her flowers as long as they'd known each other. He'd intended to give her a Christmas plant, but she'd stopped his hand on their way to the florist's. "Don't, please. It won't live," she'd insisted. No plants ever grew for her. She stared at the huge, cultivated petals of these daisies, so straight and sparkling they looked waxed—they would be awfully hard to kill in five days, and after she left no one had to know what became of them.

"Ed's a thousand miles away," she silently reminded herself. "If I'm going to make a good impression here, I'd better concentrate on being the artist again. I should be making small talk with Sharon, not thinking of Ed."

"They started hanging the show yesterday," Sharon explained as they headed for the museum. "Dave Phillips flew in from Chicago last night." Richard Calpis, the other artist, would be arriving from San Francisco that evening.

"Good," Jana thought. "I wasn't the first artist to arrive." When she curated shows, one of the worst scenarios was an out-of-town artist who had nothing better to do than supervise the hanging. Flying in early was a mark of the amateur. She recalled her first one-woman show: Buffalo, 1972. The show opened on a Thursday. Instead of shipping the paintings, Jana rented a car and drove them up on Monday, then stayed in a hotel until after the opening. Five nights in the hotel, plus the car rental, cost nearly $500. In those days her rent was $185 a month, and some months she had difficulty scraping that much together. The money would be well spent if she could be certain her work was displayed correctly, she thought. But what did she do when she got to the gallery? Stood back and watched the paintings go up, feeling out of place and afraid to open her mouth. Those days were only laughable in retrospect.

The show occupied the Walker's entire third floor; her paintings were to the left of the entrance. Electricians were busy working out the proper lighting when Jana walked in. After saying hello to a preoccupied Steve Whitman, she took a closer look around. On the wall directly opposite the elevator hung one painting by each of the three artists, along with the artists' bios and a description of the exhibition. Steve had asked which painting she felt best exemplified her motivation for the series, but she didn't realize he'd be hanging that painting on the entrance wall, or she might have thought twice about choosing *Mulberry Street*. The shadow of that murdered woman set New York in a bad light, an impression she related to Steve.

"It's difficult to cast New York City in a much worse light than it's in already," Steve said.

Jana decided to let the matter drop, but Steve's comment disturbed her. One of the excuses she'd given herself as she prepared for this show was that it would be interesting to see the different metropolitan perspectives; she'd been actually looking forward to seeing the city itself drowning out the work. Dave Phillips' work, for example, immediately reminded viewers of Chicago's polar winters—the human figures in his landscapes fighting their way out of snow drifts emerged as surreal, transformed creatures. The one time Jana had been to Chicago she'd been caught in a blizzard, and she could easily identify with what these figures were going through.

Dave seemed to have conquered the struggle between self and other which had recently been driving her crazy. Staring at his paintings, she saw past, present, and future mapped out before her: past—the outward vision channeled through internal struggles; present—inner discord transcended through close, steady observation; future—outward vision transformed by the same concentrated attention to conflict, not the painter's conflict but the subject's. Jana had mastered the outward focus years ago, at present her vision was directed inward, but eventually the two perspectives would have to merge. She might someday be able to give that woman staring out the *Mulberry Street* window a premonition of death, then paint her features the way such a premonition would distort them.

She walked around the gallery again, viewing her own work as a stage Dave might have passed through also. She was approaching her last two paintings before she caught a glimpse of herself in one of the chrome-encased spotlights: stoop-shouldered, hunched forward, gazing straight ahead at the center of every canvas. She looked more like a bag lady than an artist.

"I'm going to explore the neighborhood," she told Steve. "I'll be back in a bit." She needed air, fresh wind blowing in her face, a distance from any semblance of art. She found a little restaurant a few blocks away, sat at a table by the window, and ordered a glass of wine. She sipped it slowly, ran her fingers through her hair, relaxed a bit. One of the frustrating aspects of being in a group show, especially a show out of town, was not knowing the work of the other artists. Feeling a kinship with Dave's Chicago landscapes eased the tension. Or so she tried to convince herself. But it was more than that. She was tenser than she'd been in months, as tense as she'd been after she'd dropped off the slides at DCA. That night Ed had held her in his arms, and the tension drained out of her.

Ed, Ed, Ed, all of the sudden everything was Ed! This was ridiculous. She'd been caught in a vicious cycle lately: working at the gallery, squeezing in a little time to paint, meeting Ed for dinner. She'd lost the ability to relax alone, or with other friends. But the wine was helping. She ordered another glass, munched a handful of peanuts.

The rest of the day passed quickly. Various staff came in and out while the crew was finishing the lights—Jana went through the motions of memorizing each name, each face, but it was only when Dave entered that the introduction penetrated her professional guise. "Your paintings have a compelling immediacy," she told him.

"Thanks. I wish I could return the compliment, but I'm afraid I haven't looked closely at the show yet. My sister lives in St. Paul, and I've spent too little time with her and her family the past few years. She's been running me ragged all day." At that point Dave excused himself and walked around viewing the paintings.

Richard arrived from San Francisco at 5:30. Sharon dropped Jana off at the hotel on her way to the airport, then reminded her that a member of the museum's board of directors was throwing a dinner party at 7:00. "I'm enjoying your work," Dave mentioned in passing during the evening, but the comment was superficial. From the looks of things, there wouldn't be much chance for intense discussion. Jana consoled herself that all discussions at a time like this would be pointless—she had Dave's address and could always get in touch after things settled down. She was still digesting his work and its significance for her own work—that wasn't something she could exactly put into words yet.

⌒ ⌒

"You called at exactly the right time," Ed laughed. "I'm just about to get in bed, and I haven't the slightest idea what to wear."

Jana thought about the way he'd slept in his underpants those first nights they'd spent together. Night after night he would come in them, then get up at one or two in the morning to change. Because she was almost fanatical about his wetness seeping into her, he showered also. Many nights the hot water had been shut off, and he'd return to bed still damp, shivering, extraordinarily happy. But sleeping in his underpants now might emphasize her absence. "Why not sleep in your tuxedo?" she teased.

"You're out of your mind. Whatever would I sleep in a tux for?"

"As preparation for the gala. If APL wants to take all these mangy artists and stuff them into tuxedos, then its executives can make a few sacrifices as well. Besides, I don't want you too comfortable when I'm not around."

"Little chance of that," Ed laughed.

Jana could hear the radio in the background. "What's that doing on?" she asked. "You said you were going to bed."

"I am. I set the timer so the radio shuts off at two o'clock. That should give me time to fall asleep."

"Since when did you need anything to help you fall asleep?" She was the one who was often drinking a shot of brandy or sherry before turning in, and even then she usually lay awake for an hour listening to Ed snoring.

"I haven't needed anything since you've been around," Ed told her. "But I used to put the television on all the time when I was a kid. It drowned out my parents' voices."

"I'll be back in a few days."

"Don't be surprised if the radio wakes us up in the middle of the night."

"At least I'll know I'm missed."

"You're missed already, dear. I'm planning to make coffee and leave it for you every morning, just like always."

"You can move back to your old side of the bed tonight."

"I'd rather keep the memory of you there. Sometimes it seems as if you've been there forever."

"Doesn't it, though?" Pressing the warm phone to her ear, she told him about the flight, the museum, her excitement at seeing Dave

Phillips' work, and how it made her rethink her own direction. He told her the proofs for the exhibition catalog had come back from the printer, and during his lunch break he'd stopped by the gallery and picked up copies for Frank and Phyllis to check over.

After she hung up, Jana found herself wondering whether penguins got much sleep. Minnesota was certainly cold enough for penguins. How many people at the opening Friday would be wearing tuxedos? She was planning on wearing a gray silk pants suit, and she suddenly became worried that she'd be dreadfully out of place. This wasn't New York. For openings at The Paperworks Space and other Soho galleries, people often showed up wearing Levi's. "Dressing Up," the term Phyllis had used when she first spoke of the gala, usually meant black lace stockings, flapper dresses, red velvet jackets, or fox stoles (head attached), which the more daring wore to parties at the Palladium. She hadn't been to a black-tie affair in over ten years, and didn't relish the idea of jamming herself into an evening gown, then tripping over high heels—although maybe the tightly laced bodice would help to hold her together.

༄ ༄

Thursday passed without incident—one of the museum's board members picked up her and Richard at ten AM, drove them around to show off the town, took them out for lunch. In the afternoon there was an interview with a reporter from the *St. Paul Pioneer Press Dispatch* who was doing a feature article on the three artists. Then dinner with the museum staff, and a mediocre play at the Guthrie Theatre, across the court from the Walker. As might be expected on the day any exhibition opened, Steve and the rest of the museum staff were tied up all day Friday, and the artists were left to their own devices until the six o'clock reception. Jana walked through the enclosed downtown shopping area, looking for a souvenir she could buy for Ed. After running herself so ragged that she no longer thought to be nervous about the opening, she found the perfect gift: a small speaker that attached to the earphone jack on a Walkman—appropriate, inexpensive, and it fit easily into the suitcase.

Steve Whitman, wearing a tasteful business suit, grabbed her arm the moment she walked into the already filled gallery. She was introduced to political dignitaries; museum board members and patrons; local artists, writers, and academics; representatives from the Minnesota State Arts Board, Compas, the Jerome Foundation, and two other foundations Jana never caught the names of; the chief curator of the Walker; owners of galleries in the area; and Dave Phillips' family. Not a tuxedo in sight. The men wore suits, but here and there a sports jacket added a bit of color to the crowd; most of the women had on tailored skirts and expensive cashmere or Icelandic sweaters. "If I were the curator here, I might feel a bit out of place, but it's okay for an artist to stand out just a bit," Jana assured herself.

She struggled to recall which people she'd met before. "I'm losing my touch," she realized. "There can't be more than 200 people here. If I'm this bad now, what am I going to be like when there are 500 people at the Artistic Response to the Environment Gala?" Picturing herself having to put eighteen artists at ease, Jana was tempted to quit while she was ahead. "Ed will help," she consoled herself. The problem with Ed was that he was so at ease with people that she tended to lay back and let him make most of the small talk. Even so, at least half the people at the gala would be acquaintances whose paths crossed hers frequently, she'd have no trouble remembering them. And she'd certainly moved about with ease during recent openings at The Paperworks Space. Her tension tonight was excitement at this being her show. Still, she wished Ed were here.

"Stop wishing and start circulating," she admonished herself, smiling at the nameless face in front of her and making an effort to join in the conversation. The man standing to her left combed his prematurely white hair exactly like Ed's; she found herself drawn to him.

& &

Saturday, the fourth night away, Jana took a dime-store mystery novel to bed with her. It was a pleasure to lie back and read again, and it was a relief to sleep in her panties and a self-adhesive Modess pad. Ed kept close tabs on her menstrual cycle, and since she'd been with him she was starting to anticipate its effects herself: one month she would have cramps, the next month she'd go into a deep depression. She was in the midst of a depressed month, but the excitement of the show was enough to carry her smoothly through it. "Good thing I know there's nothing physical to be depressed about," she reminded herself. Dr. Barbash had taken another biopsy last month, and there were no further changes, so the cell structure of those warts was chalked up to her mother's probably having taken DES. She suggested Jana come for a routine examination every six months, and that was the end of it. It wasn't a contagious wart virus after all.

Ed had to practically drag her into the office for that second biopsy. "What I don't know won't hurt me," she'd insisted. Jana laughed when she imagined what she'd be like right now if she still didn't know—she'd probably exaggerate every depressing thought, every menstrual cramp would be the wart virus spreading, and Ed wouldn't be around to comfort her. When she was depressed, he held her and reminded her it was hormonal; when she had severe cramps, Ed's massaging her pubic area was the only thing that provided relief.

Jana tossed the book aside. It was the same as Dr. Waters easing her stomachaches, wasn't it? There was no use trying to deny it: every pleasurable aspect of their relationship, everything Ed did that eased the pain a little, reminded her. She placed her hand on her crotch, trying to rub out the memories. She couldn't bring back that sexual urge she'd dreamt last summer, even though it was usually strongest when she had her period. She'd been petrified of how intense it would be: five long nights alone now that she knew what it felt like to sleep with another person.

She recalled that first week after she'd lost her virginity, when she'd continually sought out mirrors in which to view herself. "I don't look any different," she'd remarked, relieved and disappointed in the same breath. She couldn't understand how she could have been through so much and not have changed a bit. "Every woman I've met in the past fifteen years experienced bodily changes when they lost their virginity because they were still teenagers at the time. Teenage bodies change every day," she'd realized, laughing at her own silliness. Jana laughed again as she remembered her expectations of a mere five months ago, but the laugh was tinged with horror: tonight she came to the realization that it had been the ability to touch herself, satisfy herself, even want herself, which had been taken away from her.

She heaved a deep sigh, flicked off the light, and pulled the covers up to her chin. She no longer knew how to stay warm by herself, either. One by one, she began listing the people who'd been at the opening yesterday, but she couldn't even remember their names. She might as well be counting those flabby sheep, one body looking precisely like the next.

No, the sheep didn't look alike, not if she looked closely and saw them for themselves instead of relying on preconceived notions. One sheep had a bit of black around his left eye, another had a black spot behind his ear, that sheep off to the left had a black muzzle. She thought of the sheep she'd seen on the farms around Yaddo—even passing in a car, she'd noticed their thin, awkward legs which didn't look sturdy enough to hold the woolly bodies. At one farm she rode by last summer, there was a horse in the same pasture; he'd picked one extremely fat sheep and was chasing it in circles. She remembered clearly now, that sheep's fur was dry and yellowed, as opposed to the pure white fur others had. She remembered seeing sheep without fur—she and Marilyn had gone up to Massachusetts a year ago last April. When the weather turned suddenly cold, the recently shorn sheep had pieces of white canvas tied around their midriffs to keep them from taking sick.

There was no use fighting it, she'd be better off getting up. Jana flicked on the light, got her robe, went over and sat cross-legged in the chair by the window, and picked up her sketch pad. Sensing the tension in her body, she drew a few circles to loosen up. She flipped the page and began drawing sheep heads, slightly more than circles themselves. Her hand moved from place to place, the heads bore no relation to each other, much like those counted sheep she'd watched arrange themselves in the pasture after they'd cleared the fence. Sometimes she drew only an ear or a neck, part of a head with lines running down to indicate the body. She drew one whole sheep which looked more like a Siberian husky.

By the time she moved to the next page she felt herself getting used to the shapes of their bodies. Her hand moved faster, the animals came out looking vaguely recognizable. She drew the grass under them, highlighted the black fur around the ear of one, the eye of another. On a new page she drew the neck and chest, then another sheep—neck, chest, and front legs. She drew a sheep with one leg raised, like a dog offering his paw to shake. She sketched a fence in front of him; the paw looked as if it was testing the height before jumping over. The sheep seemed worried, anxious. His body looked like a Siberian husky's again, only a dwarfed husky, caught in a body too big for him, his bones enormous and the fur shriveled. If he were the proper size he'd be able to make the jump easily, and he didn't understand what had happened to him.

Jana turned on the bright overhead light. She leaned the sketch pad against the wall and stared at it. Picking it up again, she extended the one raised paw until there were claws coming out of it, the hair shorn and bloody around them. She laughed at the image, and at herself; she laughed partly from the pleasure of drawing in the middle of the night, no plan, no huge project, a little off-center but comfortable.

She sat back down and drew a woman's face with shaggy black sheep hair. Then she made the face her own. "That would be an interesting hairdo," she mused: it seemed almost stylish. She turned the page and drew two women's heads, back to back, their sheep hair intertwining. Then she moved the women farther apart, until there was almost a whole sheep between them. "If I paint this, the sheep should be white," Jana realized. That would also give the women white hair. What conveyed age in women would be the sheep's normal color—it made an interesting contrast.

She drew that original sheep, the same shriveled husky body. She sketched the fence in front of him. She moved her pencil on the other side of the fence, sketching pillows, a bed. Laughing to herself, Jana imagined a woman lying there, a woman whose toenails were painted bright red, who wore a dark dull shade of lipstick and heavy blue eyeshadow even while she slept. The sheep was trying to get up to her.

On a new page she drew the outline of the bed again. She gave the woman huge breasts, placed the sheep on top of her, drew large, balloon-like paws. One paw was raised, the other sank into her breast, pressing hard, trapping her. Originally he'd intended to walk across her, but he'd been distracted by a fly buzzing around the room. Every bone in that woman's body hurt, yet she was afraid to move. The sheep doesn't need claws to imprison her, Jana realized. The terror in that woman's unseen face was obvious from the tautness of her muscles.

Still curled in the chair, Jana felt anything but tense. It was after three, and she had to get up at eight, but it should be easy to get to sleep now.

CHAPTER FOURTEEN

Wolf in Sheep's Clothing

AT FOUR O'CLOCK on Monday, Jana stepped off the plane, and there was Ed waiting for her. He'd gotten a piece of poster board and written REPLANSKY on it, like the limousine drivers carried. With one of her pastels, he'd drawn a flower in the corner. She fell into his arms, hardly believing her eyes.

Yes, she'd been missed. "It's sometimes so comfortable when we're together that I find myself taking you for granted," he told her. They needed to spend more quiet, passionate time with each other. Tonight he planned to make up for lost time—he'd take her back to the apartment, carry her over the threshold and straight into the bedroom. "I've got a bottle of wine breathing on the table, and dinner just has to be popped in the oven—filet of sole wrapped around asparagus with hollandaise sauce." They'd work so hard at loving that they'd both be famished.

"Sounds fantastic." Jana pushed through the crowd to get a better view as the bags began circling. "I haven't eaten since breakfast."

It was almost five by the time they got out of the parking lot; most of the traffic was headed in the other direction, but driving through the city created an edge of tension that put thoughts of ravishing his girlfriend on the back burner. They walked in, poured wine, and Ed put the fish in the oven and boiled water for noodles. Everything in due time, he told himself, glad simply to have her home with him.

At last they finished eating. Ed put the dishes in the sink to soak while Jana began unpacking. She appeared at the kitchen door a moment later, holding up the sketch of the sheep standing confused before the fence.

"Where'd that come from?"

"Minnesota. I started counting sheep, and he just came out. It's a wolf in sheep's clothing."

"So I noticed. Anybody we know?"

"I'm not quite sure. I think it's someone who has sheepskin covers over his car seats," Jana teased. "Someone who's been looking a little woolly lately."

"Are my teeth that big?"

"Right now they are."

Ed grinned. "Remember what happened to Red Riding Hood," he cautioned as he lunged toward her.

"Remember what happened to the *wolf*." She fended him off for a moment until she could put the drawing safely away. "Your teeth aren't the only thing that have gotten so big, I notice," she said, turning back to him.

"The better to love you with, my dear." He led her toward the couch.

"Is that really what the wolf did?"

Ed didn't answer; his head was buried in her hair as she curled against him. Neither could seem to get close enough. Just as he was about to suggest they get rid of these awkward garments and move this same configuration to the bedroom, Jana jumped up.

"If you think the wolf's good, wait till you see the drawings I did after I got him out of my system," she said, rushing to get her portfolio. Ed stayed slumped on the couch where she'd left him, too stunned to move, while Jana presented an endless display of drawings. "So what do you think?" she asked.

"I think I want you back here." He tapped the cushion beside him.

"I'll be back in a moment. But seriously, Ed, how do you like the drawings? I think I've really broken through to something. . ."

"What is this, some kind of test? If my reaction's appropriate, you'll sleep with me?"

"What the hell ? . ."

"You're a cockteaser, you know that?"

"You're out of your mind. All I wanted was to show you a few drawings I'm excited about."

"Go call Gary! He's a better critic than I am."

"I don't want a critic, I want a lover."

"You only think you do."

"Don't tell me what I *think*, please," Jana said as she started toward the phone. "I'm sorry if I spoiled your romantic moment, but to tell the truth, it wasn't very romantic to begin with."

"Excuse me! I thought you wanted a man who would take things slowly,"

"Slow, sure. But you take forever, when you have energy to do anything at all."

"Look who's talking. You're so involved in your work you're not even aware when I walk into a room sometimes."

"You sound just like my parents. When I lived with them I *had* to be accommodating, but I'll be damned if I'm going to drop everything because you want a glass of water. If I let the process be interrupted, I lose the inspiration, and the work's ruined. I've told you that a thousand times."

"You use *inspiration* as an excuse for everything, don't you?"

"It's not an excuse, it's my life."

"But it doesn't *have* to be." Ed grabbed her arm. "All I'm asking is for you to love me, pure and simple. Look at me! Sure, my hair's white, but I'm not Dr. Waters. I'm not seventy years old. I'm with you because I love you, not because there's no one else in my life. And I'm not trying to take advantage of you. But you've got to trust me, Jana. Don't you even care enough about me to let go of the artist for a few minutes?" He stepped in front of her, ready to scoop her up in his arms again.

"No, I don't!" Jana screamed, turning away and shoving the sketchbook back into her portfolio. "You seem to be forgetting, I *am* an artist."

"And what am I, a chauffeur?"

"Nobody told you to pick me up at the airport."

"Pardon me. I *thought* I was picking up my girlfriend!"

"I'm *myself*. I can't just fall into some role you expect from a woman."

"You're the one playing roles, my dear! One minute you're loving, the next minute you're playing Little Miss Art Snob and treating me like a groupie or something. I want to be supportive in all aspects of your life, but I can't just sit back and let you abuse me."

Jana had no comeback for that one. She slumped down on the sofa and stared off into space. What could she tell him—that lately the roles had been getting confused for her, too? That sometimes she found herself wanting to go back to the uncomplicated life she'd had before she'd met him, when all that was expected of her were the demands she made on herself? That she didn't know who she was anymore, she felt herself losing control? "I don't mean to be abusing you," she said weakly. "And I'm certainly not aware when I'm doing that. Sometimes I catch myself snapping at something you say, and I have no idea why."

"I know that," Ed said, sitting down beside her, close but not touching. "I'm aware this is your first relationship, and that it's confusing at times. I try to be patient, but you have to realize there's a limit." Almost in tears, he shifted his head away. She was hard to understand sometimes. For over six months they'd spent every night together; if she went through any changes, he'd be the first to notice, and he couldn't help feeling slighted now. That sheep resembled a stuffed animal, yet she didn't even seem to realize their conversation about stuffed animals might have prompted the drawing. Whatever he said or did seemed of no importance anymore.

"So you're counting sheep, are you?" he asked. It was the only safe thing he could think to say. It reminded him of when he used to sleep at Kathe's. Near the end, when she had only two or three dogs left, she often let them sleep on the bed. If he was there, they'd come around to his side and whine to be picked up. He'd pick up one then another would cry, the first would jump off then cry to be picked up again, and so on through the night, an endless stream of little dogs crying to be picked up. It was the closest he ever came to counting sheep. And who knows, maybe Jana's obsession with her career was as bad as Kathe and her dogs after all.

He sat there holding her for a few minutes then softly asked if he could see the drawings again.

"Not now," Jana responded. "I'm exhausted. I just want to get to bed."

They gave in and lay side by side on the freshly laundered sheets. Tired as she was, Jana quickly found her mind churning. She tried one position, then another. In her few days away the bed seemed to have become lopsided, Ed's side sinking further than her own—she found it hard to keep her balance.

Ed's heavy body motioned toward the foreign object beside him; he lifted his head off the pillow. "Oh, I forgot to tell you—Natalie called last night."

"I know, she was confused about when I was coming back. She reached me at the hotel."

"What did she want?"

"Some complication about one artist coming to town. I didn't get the details—I'll deal with it tomorrow." Jana turned away from him, fluffed the pillow under her. She had half a mind to get up, go out to the living room, and work. Only she didn't exactly want to draw. "I'm probably overtired," she mumbled aloud.

"And you have every right to be." He went on to lecture her about how important it was that she get a good night's sleep: she had to go into the gallery tomorrow, there was probably a stack of work waiting for her. "It's always hard getting back to work after a vacation," Ed whispered, running his hand along her back.

"No, it's not. I mean, it never used to be. Besides, this wasn't a vacation." She lay silently, swallowing her tears. "Sometimes I think I'm no good to anyone, including myself, unless I'm painting, and right now I don't feel very much like an artist," she told him. "I come home all excited about new perspectives I want to work toward, and instead of getting down to work I have to go play curator tomorrow." Instead of getting down to work, Ed expected her to make love to him. Wearing two hats was bad enough, but three was impossible. Small wonder she was getting the roles confused.

"You *are* an artist," Ed assured her. "A three-person show at the Walker is nothing to scoff at. And you're turning down other shows— what about that woman who wanted to give you a show in New York last month? I don't understand why you didn't want..."

"I don't need another line on my resume." Jana pulled away from him. She stared up at the ceiling as she talked. "Audrey would give me a show, she'd put up the paintings, although last time she didn't even manage that very well—instead of hiring union workers, she arranged for some art student to hang it. An hour before he was due at the gallery he called to say he was involved in a painting and couldn't make it. The two of us worked till two AM, and I was a wreck at the opening. And once the show's up, Audrey won't do anything else for me—she won't bother to get out press releases, she won't get in touch with critics, the gallery doesn't even have a list of regular patrons."

"What's preventing you from calling the critics yourself? You certainly know plenty of them; you and Natalie are constantly taking critics out to dinner. And it would be a chance for all my friends to see your work."

"It's not the artist's job to get in touch with the right people, and artists who push too hard aren't respected. If I had a show with Audrey, it would cost over $1,000 to get everything framed, plus all the time and energy that would go into preparations, and I wouldn't get enough in return. At this point, it might even be detrimental. I can just hear Nancy Hoffman now: Why, darling, I'd truly been planning a show for you next fall, but you've just had a show, haven't you? We must not flood the market. You of all people understand that, don't you, dear?"

Ed laughed at her impersonation; he'd never met Nancy Hoffman, but he could just imagine what she must be like. It was a forced laugh, though. He was laughing to cover his initial anger and embarrassment at Jana's treating him as if he didn't know the first thing about marketing artwork. He told himself again she didn't realize what she was saying, or how the words affected him. He tightened his grip on her. He tried to let his muscles speak all the tension and love he had in him, but his body lost its hold. Jana settled her head on his chest and drifted off to sleep. It was Ed who lay awake, feeling a surge of delight that she had fallen asleep at last in such a trusting position, that she had, indeed, returned home to him. Long after she rolled over onto her own side of the bed, he lay awake rehashing everything that had happened this evening. He fixed the sheet so it covered his nostrils, to make sure she wouldn't waken from his breathing, then lay there guarding her sleep for as long as he could.

❧ ❧

"You're *what?*" Ed backed away from the phone.

"I'm going back to my place after I finish up at the gallery. I need to be alone for a while."

"So what time will you be over? Do you want to wait and have a late dinner, or would you rather eat alone?"

"Ed, I'm saying I won't be over. Or I don't think I will. It's hard to think straight. As I said, I need some time alone."

"You haven't even been back for twenty-four hours."

"Well, then, it should be easier for you to adjust to my being away."

"You're still upset about last night, aren't you? Look, I said a lot of things I didn't mean. Anger does strange things to people."

"I know; I said a lot of things I didn't mean, too. That's why I want to be alone for a few nights, to sort things through."

"Where does that leave me, if I may ask?"

"Oh, come on, Ed, we've never structured our whole lives around each other. I'll give you a call in a day or two, okay?"

"Have it your way," Ed said. "I may or may not be home." This wasn't the sort of conversation he wanted to be having from work, but on second thought, at least the office environment prevented him from telling her what he really thought. At times like this, he wondered if she was worth the effort. He was starting to understand his father better, to realize why his father worked late, or on other nights walked away from his mother's "dizzy spells."

Jana brushed his anger aside; there were too many other tasks requiring her attention, like that artist from Los Angeles who'd phoned while she was in Minneapolis.

"Oh, thank God you called," the harried voice so different from Ed's began. "I've got to change my plane reservations. I don't believe it, but the college won't let me reschedule my Wednesday evening Art in Life class, which means I can't get out of here until Thursday morning." She went on, complaining about having to teach Art in Life for the third term in a row, how jealous her colleagues were about anyone with a career off-campus. Here she was in a major exhibition and they couldn't care less.

Jana stared hollowly around her and realized that, no matter what was going on with Ed, at least she was in better shape than a lot of other people. She went through all the necessary calming motions, then called Phyllis Mason's office. She explained the situation to Phyllis' assistant, who promised to get the departure date changed on the tickets, then call and give the artist the new flight number.

Most of the other things piled up at the gallery were equally trivial, but Jana busied herself there until after eight. Then, remembering she'd more than likely have free time tonight, she threw the guest list for the gala into her pocketbook, wanting to check it over one more time before the invitations went out.

Niels was walking down the stairs as Jana entered her building. "Where in the world have you been hiding yourself?" he asked the moment he saw her.

"Working," Jana said. Niels hadn't been in her apartment since she'd returned to the city last September, had he? That day Ed had picked her up at the bus station. They used to sit around talking, gossiping, and drinking once a month at least. "We're putting on this huge city-wide exhibition, and it's driving me crazy," she continued.

"The environment exhibition? That *is* yours, then—I thought I recognized the name of the gallery. I've seen your posters all over the city."

"Great," Jana smiled. "That means our media blitz is working."

"I guess you *are* going to be in town over the next few weeks, aren't you? I'm in a play in Cincinnati, of all places, from May 15 to June 22. I didn't see you around and was worried I'd have to ask that awful Mrs. Horowitz to take in my mail. You know she reads everything. I'd come back to find that how much I owed on my Visa card was neighborhood information."

Jana laughed at Niels' description of their neighbor, finding his effeminate gestures a refreshing contrast to the macho act Ed had pulled last night. "I'll be in town, and I'll be happy to take the mail in," she said. "I'll probably be working like crazy till the exhibition opens May 30, but if you don't catch me around, slide the keys under my door, okay?"

They chatted a few more minutes before Jana found an appropriate chance to say how exhausted she was and to apologize for not being a good neighbor lately. "As soon as you return from Cincinnati we'll have dinner," she promised. It *would* be fun to sit around with him, but before she could relax with Niels, or anyone else, she needed time alone with her art again.

She shoved a slightly bent key in the mailbox lock. Who picked up her mail while she was away this time? Ed, of course. He'd gone out of his way to come over here. Running into Niels tonight couldn't have been better timed to prove she didn't have to be so reliant on her lover, or whatever he was. Hurriedly she flipped through the envelopes in her hand—nothing but bills. She was still waiting for that check from Blue Cross; she'd paid Dr. Barbash months ago and hadn't been reimbursed yet. She should be lucky she was getting anything back—this individual insurance policy cost over $2,000 per year and provided rotten coverage. Besides taking forever to reimburse a claim, they were continually sending her half what she was expecting, along with a note stating it was the maximum allotted for a particular treatment. She would have to work for a large company in order to get decent insurance, someplace like APL. She'd have no trouble paying the medical bills if she and Ed were married, she thought sourly.

"I *must* be overtired if I can think such thoughts," she admonished herself. By the time she climbed the steep flight of stairs to her apartment, she was too exhausted to think about anything, let alone work. Disgusted with the world, she took every animal out of her closet, tossed them on the bed, and plopped down in the midst of them. The turtle felt brittle against her neck; the pig's eyes glared at her. She threw the other animals off and lay back with Leroy in her arms. She could barely feel his leg between her thighs; she probably hadn't restuffed him as well as she thought she had. All she'd tried to do was get him clean. Was it such a crime to have wanted a perfect lion?

She placed his other leg next to the first. That was better, but now his head hit her breast at an awkward, uncomfortable angle. She maneuvered the head out of the way and braced her chin on one paw. No matter what she did he seemed to placidly accept it. But she was used to someone responding now, she was used to someone cuddling back and sometimes surprising her with a kiss or a tickling finger.

Why hadn't she thought to take the ribbon off Leroy's neck? She was going to ruin it, but she was too tired to get up now. As she was about to drift off to sleep, she felt his fur hot against her; she rolled over, unconsciously abandoning the lion just as she abandoned Ed at night. Leroy was still there when she woke, his motionless body locking her against the wall.

She glanced at her watch: 9:45. That's the nice thing about living alone, Jana reminded herself, she could sleep when she wanted, paint when she wanted. So long as she put in her day at the gallery, the rest of her time was her own. She could get up and paint right now, without giving a second thought to what Ed considered a respectable bedtime. And when she was finished she could leave the canvas set up, she didn't have to feel like a little kid told to put away her toys because Mommy and Daddy were expecting company. Her space was her own here, no one would be looking over her shoulder. She didn't have to feel guilty about using inspiration "as an excuse," as Ed so bluntly put it. It felt good to be home again.

She pulled the drawing of the sheep on a woman's chest out of her portfolio. Yes, she told herself, that woman knew what it felt like to be trapped; locked against the wall by a sheep, a plush lion, or a human lover, it made no difference. She placed a primed canvas on her easel and set to work in a dazed fury which might have frightened her if she hadn't chalked it up to just waking from a nap. She painted the woman's chest on the white sheet, brown, white, brown, white, applying the paints fresh from their containers, using the canvas like a palette to blend the colors. A circle for her head, then full, mountainous breasts. She dipped one of the smaller brushes in red paint and drew a line dividing the breasts, then a small square above the line, dabs of paint beneath it.

The weight on that woman's chest appeared overbearing, it reminded Jana of an open wound, a woman bleeding to death. Herself perhaps. "You have to paint into your fear, not give way to it," Harriman used to tell his beginners classes. She lunged forward, dipped the brush again. Without bothering to scrape off the excess, she went over the line quickly but carefully. She let it dry for a minute, then repeated the process. Now it had a thick, velvetlike texture, but the image was even more horrific.

Exhausted, Jana lay back on the bed. It had been a long time since she'd gotten so worn out by painting. Unconsciously, she gripped her crotch. She felt the same sensation as when she'd sat alone staring out the window at Yaddo last summer, the bodily sense of missing Ed. "Don't you even care enough about me to let go of the artist for a few minutes?" Ed's harsh words rang in her ears. Last night, her response had been so quick, so cut and dried: "No, I don't!" She twisted Leroy's long tail around her wrist, unwound it and twisted it around the other direction. "I guess I care more than I realized," she admitted aloud. Painting was a part of her life, but it was no longer her *whole* life. The work on that canvas might have been intense, but it wasn't enough to get her through the night.

The phone was right by the bed, all she had to do was reach for it, what was she waiting for? She picked up the receiver and pounded Ed's numbers. She asked if it was too late for her to come over. She was trembling, shivering, shaking as she did some nights in his arms.

"Oh, for God's sake, make up your mind!" Ed said brusquely. Jana gasped. "Okay, look, I didn't mean that as harshly as it sounded. Of course you can still come over. And take a cab—it's nearly midnight."

She put the phone down quickly, before she could say "I love you" or "I miss you" or anything that corny. She closed the paint jars tightly, turned the still-wet canvas to face the wall, then picked up a tarp and threw it over the easel for good measure. The paint was liable to smear, but at the moment that seemed like it might be the best answer. The last thing she needed was to meet this monstrosity head-on next time she came in here.

"Maybe I'll feel more comfortable if I bring a nightgown," Jana mused as she hunted for the keys she'd hurriedly thrown into her pocketbook. Some part of her still wanted to keep a distance from Ed. But she didn't even know where she'd put that nightgown she'd bought in Saratoga last summer. It was enough to have found her keys.

That nightgown never felt comfortable, she reminded herself as she crawled into a cab. She'd have been better off buying silk pajamas, like the Chinese pair she'd brought to camp. They were incredible—black bottoms with an orange and black print top that had thick ribbon ties instead of buttons. The kids in her bunk had gotten angry with her for losing points in the volleyball game and put some sort of oatmeal mixture between the sheets of her cot; it was only the second time she'd worn those pajamas, and they'd been ruined.

The girl in the cot next to hers had a blue gingham nightgown with a little stuffed dog to match. All Jana had was polyester baby dolls and that red velvet dachshund her parents had sent. It was the stupidest-looking dog she'd ever seen, bright red with black ears and a pipe cleaner tail, not even a foot long, less substantial than a Coney Island hot dog. She'd written home saying she wanted a *small* stuffed animal, meaning that the teddy bears from when she was younger were too large, too dirty, embarrassing—but she didn't mean *that* small. It had to be big enough for the other kids to notice, maybe an autograph hound like older girls had. As if anyone in her bunk would have signed for her.

At last the cab reached Ed's building. Jana shoved a ten dollar bill through the grate and rushed out without asking for change, anxious to curl up in his arms and forget everything. She needed to be held, touched in ways she'd hadn't known about a year ago. Whatever problems there might be between her and Ed, it was better than being alone with the memories.

Thank God he didn't want to talk about their conversation today. He'd been half asleep when she'd called and now, an hour later, he snored lightly beside her. She placed one arm under the pillow and wondered what had become of that dachshund. She'd left him standing on the cot when she went home earlier than planned. She hadn't bothered to bring him to the infirmary, either. What did she expect him to do, bark at Dr. Waters? How could a red velvet dog protect her?

Red velvet—precisely what that line in the painting had made her think of! No wonder she'd been frightened by the image. Maybe Ed was right, maybe she should have begun painting stuffed animals years ago. Maybe then that stupid dog wouldn't have snuck up on her like all the other camp memories.

She never wanted to paint again. She wanted to never be alone again, to never again use her art to assuage loneliness. No, that wasn't what she felt—when the work was going well it nourished her. The problem was that she wasn't sure she *could* be alone again, wasn't sure she'd be able to paint without being scared off. She'd been working toward transformation but hadn't planned on giving up control, and suddenly, loss of control became terrifying.

Even Ed's presence in the bed tonight proved harrowing. He slept restlessly. Jana kept flashing on his shocked, sleepy head as it turned to her and found her still awake. She was terrified he was going to wake up completely, turn over, and jab it in her.

Jab it in her! Jana clenched her eyes at the words. Always she'd been terrified of being jabbed—when she was too little to swallow a pill, her mother used to threaten that, if she didn't take the medicine like a good girl, the doctor was going to come in the middle of the night, wake her up, and give her a shot. Just jab the needle in her. Dr. Waters had threatened to give her a needle, too, hadn't he? At the infirmary, the first time, the time she was honestly sick. Ed. . .

But Ed's body was turned away from her. She lay back again, thinking over the day's events, then the week's events, then the month's events. She was starting to feel nauseous. She got up and made her way silently into the bathroom.

As long as he was awake, Ed was sensitive to her every movement: a twitch of her muscles unsettled him, and he would explore her body searching for the tiny area that was feeling, perhaps, unloved. But the moment he fell asleep he closed off to her—she sighed or coughed while he snored to cover these interferences. One night, two weeks ago, she'd gotten nauseous before Ed fell asleep. He called out once to see if she was okay, then turned over and buried his head in the pillow. Faking sick to get attention, or sometimes actually getting sick, was what Kathe used to do, begging him to soothe the pain another man had caused her.

There wasn't much Ed could do, Jana rationalized between bouts of choking. She flashed on childhood nights, alone in her room, when she would cry, softly at first, then gradually louder, waiting to see how long it would take her parents to come in. They heard her every time.

The effort to muffle her choking made her feel worse. Jana sat on the toilet seat, shivering and sweating at the same time, hoping she'd be able to get up, turn around, and aim for the toilet bowl. She didn't make it. One quick stream of vomit on the tile floor, a bit on the bath mat. She went into the kitchen, got cleanser, tore off several paper towels, went back and cleaned it as best she could, returned the cleanser to its place under the sink, washed off somewhat, patted herself dry. Ed was liable to waken if her body was wet and sticky, and it was too late for him to help her now.

She crawled back into bed, lined her back up rigidly against Ed's, tried to get comfortable. She slept off and on, a deep sleep for maybe an hour, the rest haunted by dreams she seemed to play no role in. She was wide awake when Ed's alarm went off, but remained motionless, her eyes closed. She got up the moment she heard the door lock.

დ დ

She wasn't due at the gallery until eleven—plenty of time to relax this morning. She was drinking her second cup of coffee when she decided to check over that guest list. It wasn't in her pocketbook. Damn, it must have fallen out when she was searching for her keys last night. She ought to stop home and get it, she supposed. She didn't want to leave Ed alone again this evening, and there was no telling how late she'd be tied up at the gallery.

Jana grabbed a cab across town. She retrieved the guest list and shoved it in her pocketbook. She intended to step around the easel as she headed for the bathroom, but found herself mysteriously drawn to it. "Oh, for God's sake," she admonished herself. "What is this, *the Portrait of Dorian Gray*?" It was sheer insanity to allow one painting to haunt her.

She bit her bottom lip and pulled the tarp off, then turned the canvas toward her. Wow! It was like seeing a stranger's work. The beige and white strokes held a surprising energy, yet they emanated from a still center. That woman's chest seem to be throbbing with anxiety bordering on ecstasy. Of all her recent paintings, this might even be the strongest. And the red line? If she insisted upon pigeonholing it, it could be a heart as easily as anything else.

CHAPTER FIFTEEN

Vista

"THERE HE IS." Marsha spotted Ed near the entrance to the Vista Hotel ballroom and approached with the program director for a dance company which had recently received funding. "Ed's put a lot of extra effort into this exhibition, and we'll have him to thank if our board of directors appropriates more money for arts-related expenditures in the near future," she said by way of introduction.

"It's extremely impressive," the woman to Marsha's left said. "I'm continually going to charity and publicity functions, but this is the first one in years I've *enjoyed.* You're not forcing art down people's throats, you're giving them space to appreciate it. Even the opening ceremonies were concise and appropriate."

Ed smiled and asked noncommittal questions about the dance programs the company planned for the coming year. He wasn't used to hearing Marsha—or, more importantly, Frank—praising him for the success of a program he'd recommended for funding. Although he told himself he was happy mainly for Jana's sake, he was looking forward to working with other arts organizations. He wanted to see, feel, *smell* new projects taking shape. He'd always wanted to do the best job he could, but suddenly he envisioned unprecedented returns from his efforts. A successful community arts project seemed to subconsciously enrich people's lives. They didn't flock to view it, often they didn't notice it, and yet it had its effect. Yesterday afternoon he'd dropped by Lincoln Center just after the show had been hung, and felt an aura of serenity hovering above the crowd. Tomorrow it might be a harried worker or shopper slightly calmed by drawings on the walls of the Herald Center. Next month perhaps a child would laugh at the mime performing on a street corner, part of another arts project APL was sponsoring this summer.

A few feet away from where he was standing, a photographer from the *Times* clustered Frank, Natalie, and Ed Koch together for a picture. Ed understood Frank's inclusion in the photo to be one more point in his favor—executives who work for the corporate sponsors were usually cut from the focus. The smile on Phyllis' face as she stood beside the photographer assured him he wasn't the only person aware of this little triumph.

He watched Jana flit from one group of people to another. "What's your secret?" he asked when they found themselves alone for a split second. "You're more of a charmer than Phyllis is tonight, and it's her *job* to be charming."

"Maybe it's the extra rush of adrenalin," she said. "When I start to speak, the right words come out. To tell the truth, I hadn't realized."

"Don't be so quick to discredit it," Ed cautioned as she moved gracefully on to the next conversation. Was this the same woman who paced the apartment last night, worried that the gala wouldn't go well, that she'd find herself off in a corner like she did at the parties she'd gone to when she first moved to New York? Her description of those days had been so vivid she'd almost convinced him. Tonight she exhibited the same confidence and ease he'd been attracted by the first time they met, talking to Frank one minute, to Marilyn the next, to some man or woman unknown to him the next. Now she led a tall, thin man who reminded him of Abraham Lincoln in his direction.

"This is Lou Daniels," Jana said as she introduced him. "I was just telling Lou that you saw his show at The Paperworks Space last year."

"I most certainly did," Ed said, reaching out to shake Lou's hand. "Your drawings not only made a strong impression, they convinced me that The Paperworks Space was the right gallery to work with on this project." Smiling to himself, he recalled the events of that afternoon— the first time he and Jana had been alone. A quick glance at Jana revealed she was thinking the same thing. "That show also convinced me I'd found the perfect curator," he added, drawing Jana close to him.

"So Jana tells me," Lou said, laughing. "Always glad to be of use. That show was my first in the Big Apple, and I hoped it would lead to bigger things, but I never dreamed something like this was in the works."

"At the time, neither did I," Jana insisted, smiling up at Ed.

Ed was called over to meet someone Frank and Marsha were talking to. Jana turned around to find Marilyn behind her. "Are you certain you curated this exhibition?" Marilyn asked in greeting. "You seem much calmer tonight than you are at openings at The Paperworks Space."

"There's something to be said for working through the City of New York," Jana laughed. "I wasn't allowed to drive a single nail. If you're going to curate a show, I'm learning you might as well go for broke—I didn't get any more frazzled supervising the hanging of a hundred drawings than I do hanging ten, and there wasn't time to stand there staring at the lighting or getting myself worked up over trivialities."

"I have a feeling other elements of your life entered into this," Marilyn said. "You and Ed make a great couple."

"That's precisely what Natalie told me a year ago. I don't know whether to laugh or cry hearing it from *you* now."

"Natalie and I have a right to agree once in a while, even if we don't use the same methods to draw conclusions. Seriously, you seem radiant. I've never seen you look so good."

"Thanks. I've been feeling pretty good, too—emotionally *and* physically." Jana squeezed Marilyn's hand as she excused herself, promising to call early next week. She'd talked to Marilyn several times that week when she was upset about the possibility of a wart virus, but every time they'd talked since then she'd been so caught up in talking about the show at the Walker or what was going on with the exhibition that she'd never told Marilyn the final verdict on those "warts." After next week I'll have time for friends again, she reminded herself as she hastened over to an artist who'd been standing behind Marilyn trying to get her attention.

Word had gotten out that dinner would be served soon, and people began hunting for their placards and taking their designated seats. Jana searched the crowd for Ed, spotted him over by the far wall, and started toward him, then pulled up short as she drew near. She'd noticed from the distance that he was talking with Bill Fitch, but now she saw Matt Fillmore standing next to Bill. The three men were heavily involved in conversation. All Jana could think was "let me out of here!" But it was too late—both Bill and Ed had spotted her. Here it comes, she thought, taking one step at a time. Ed's going to make some asinine political comment, he and Matt are going to get into an argument, and I'm going to have to back Matt up. As curator, it's my duty to stand behind my artists.

Besides, my views are probably closer to Matt's than Ed's. Ed and I will probably spend all night arguing once we get home—assuming we even go home together. She took another step and found herself standing at Bill's side.

"Quite a speech the mayor gave," Bill was saying. "I wasn't expecting Koch to speak out against toxic waste as strongly as he did. I was at a dinner where John Harrington spoke last month, and he seemed to be carefully avoiding controversial issues."

"Who?" Jana asked.

"John S. Harrington, Reagan's Energy Secretary, such as he is."

"New York City has a Democratic administration," Ed said. "Most Democrats are willing to take a stand on environmental issues."

"So our city's willing to take a stronger stand than APL is, right?" Matt asked. There was a threatening edge of mockery in his voice. Jana could no longer pretend Matt didn't know who he was talking to.

"We sponsored the exhibition, didn't we?" Ed laughed back. "Besides, APL is accountable to its stockholders. Koch is only accountable to the voters, and this isn't an election year." Bill and Jana laughed; Matt held his ground. "I stopped by Lincoln Center yesterday," Ed continued. "Your drawings make a strong impression."

"Too strong for you?" Matt asked. This time even Bill glared at him.

"Have you seen the show yet?" Bill asked.

"Can't say as I have," Matt admitted. "So how's the plaque look?" He let a brief grin cross his face.

"The drawings look better, that's for sure," Ed told him.

Matt seemed to be trying to read between the lines of Ed's face. Well, Jana realized, there were a few more wrinkles than she'd noticed before. "Just because someone represents a company doesn't mean he shares all their views," Bill commented. "Off the record, of course."

"Right, free speech and all that," Matt laughed. He promised to stop by and see the show over the weekend. "Let's face it, you're serving damn good champagne, it's the least I can do," he said, raising his glass on leaving. Jana, Ed, and Bill stood watching him head for his table, then burst out laughing. They got through it, Jana told herself—Ed had handled himself magnificently, not compromising APL and not embarrassing her. No wonder she loved him.

Jana surveyed the rest of the room as she and Ed walked toward Table 2. At the ribbon-cutting ceremonies, the artists had shyly clustered together, but now, loosened by champagne, she watched them introducing themselves as they sat down next to social register couples who regularly supported the arts. She recalled a friend of her father's, a successful stockbroker, who insisted that he played golf solely for business reasons. Who knew what deals might be arranged tonight while waiting for the second or third course to be served?

Natalie was seated with Frank Markowitz and his wife, at a table shared by Ed Koch, Bess Myerson (the other keynote speaker), plus various members of APL's board of directors. Jana and Ed shared the next table with two artists and members of The Paperworks Space board. Diners had their choice of steak Dijon or a shrimp and scallop casserole that was a Vista specialty. A bowl in which orange and white lilies floated was centered on every table.

Ed struck up a conversation with Gary and Larry Rivers, drawing them out on their perspectives about the recently initiated "Percent for Art" program, by which corporations pledged a percentage of their profits toward arts funding at the beginning of each fiscal year. Jana listened almost with envy—given the slightest encouragement, Larry elaborated upon his views until he turned even enthusiasts against themselves, but Gary was reserved and usually withdrawn, especially when his wife was with him. And here was Ed, meeting them both for the first time, knowing the history of her aborted romance with Gary, chatting away as if he'd known them for years. He wasn't making inane comments like "Maybe you'd like to do some drawings in time for the exhibition," but participating in an informed, stimulating dialogue.

The conversation continued through soup and salad, into the main course. As dinner plates were being collected, the Buck Clayton Band began playing one of Duke Ellington's songs. "I haven't heard this swing sound since I was a kid, but it's wonderful to hear it again," someone at the next table commented. "Where did you dream up a band like this?" Not waiting for Natalie's response, Jana beamed in Ed's direction. Her lover had, as always, made a good choice. A dozen couples got up to dance, and Jana was enchanted by the colors of their flowing skirts. She recalled teasing Ed about sleeping in a tuxedo two months ago, then hanging up the phone and giving free rein to her insecurities about dressing up tonight. Now she caught herself enjoying watching the women blend with drapes and flowers, creating a fairy tale spectacle.

Ed placed his hand over hers. It wasn't until he whispered "perfect beat" that Jana realized she'd been tapping her fingers on the table. They'd been to two previous dinner dances, and each time Ed asked her to dance she'd used the excuse that she had no sense of rhythm. The room was noisy, she had to keep one eye out for people coming over to congratulate her on the exhibition or to just say hello, and yet tonight her subconscious was hearing the music perfectly. Smiling, gracious, grace-*ful,* and relaxed enough to let the evening proceed in whatever way it would, she let Ed lead her onto the highly polished dance floor.

ری ری

"Give me a hand with this, will you?" Jana made quite a sight, standing barefoot in the bedroom doorway. Her left arm was over her shoulder, elbow out at the side like a pathetic chicken wing, her right arm stretched backward as she leaned forward. She'd somehow managed to get her zipper halfway down; now neither hand could reach it.

"Oh, for God's sake," Ed said, purposely taking his time coming over. "I can't take you anywhere," he jokingly protested.

"I took you," Jana said, standing upright and feeling her blood settle away from her head. She shouldn't have drunk so much.

Ed eased the zipper down. Jana stepped out of the evening gown that had held her captive all night. They both breathed easier, then burst out laughing. "What would you do without me?" Ed teased.

"Don't tempt me, or I just might curate that show in California." One of the guests tonight was a member of Reagan's Task Force for the Environment. He'd told Jana several times how impressive the exhibition was, and mentioned that he was "checking it out" for a close friend who worked in the funding office of a Los Angeles power company. If this show was successful, they were thinking of staging something similar on "the coast." Praising the works Jana had selected once again, he asked if he could give his friend her name and recommend her as a guest curator.

"Promises, promises," Ed laughed. If he continued talking, Jana didn't hear him. She was in the bathroom, washing the makeup off her face with handfuls of warm water. Yes, makeup. She'd let Natalie talk her into it. "After all, there will be TV cameras, and with no color you'll look all washed out," Nat had said. Jana glanced toward the shower, but felt incapable of showering tonight—more than likely the soap would slip away from her. Just as the clock struck three, she slid into bed.

"You *could* curate that show, you know," Ed said as he enfolded her in his arms.

Jana expected him to break out laughing a moment later, but the laughter never came. "Don't be ridiculous," she said, moving away from him to fluff her pillow. "I can't abandon my painting."

"Who said you had to abandon painting? I'm sure there are plenty of workspaces available in Los Angeles."

"Okay, then I'd be abandoning *you*." She poked him in the chest on the word *you*.

"No, you wouldn't. I don't easily feel abandoned; I'm stronger than you think," Ed laughed. "If a relationship's going to fall apart because one person takes off for two or three months, then it wasn't much good to begin with. Besides, we're talking about a few years down the road. Maybe I'd be able to take a few months off by then, or I could fly out on alternate weekends. Anything's possible."

The words rang in Jana's ears: *anything's possible*. It was, wasn't it? Who would have dreamed a year ago, even three months ago, that the exhibition would come off this smoothly, that she'd be back at her own work despite all the pressure at the gallery, despite what Ed now teasingly referred to as his "intrusions." Who would have guessed two months ago that she'd be comfortably lying here with Ed, without regretting that she wasn't home painting, not aware of any conflicts whatsoever. They'd probably be lying in this same position two or three years down the road. And if they weren't, it wouldn't be the end of the world. People changed, they grew together and apart, but change was nothing to be afraid of.

Jana turned over. The large wooden rocking chair that had once belonged to Ed's grandmother swayed gently in the breeze from the open window. Her robe and Ed's were thrown over the back of it, more carelessly than usual tonight. The belt from her robe lay across Leroy's legs, almost like a seatbelt. "No more closets for *this* lion," Ed had declared on the spur of the moment one night when he'd picked Jana up at her studio. She had opened her closet to get some summer clothes out, and Ed had spotted Leroy looking rather sad in a corner. Reluctantly, Jana agreed Leroy belonged out in the open, if only to make sure he never snuck up on her the way that dachshund had. "He'll be like our child," Ed declared. And giddy as new parents always are, they brought him home together. Poor battered Leroy; he might not be perfect but, if anything, they loved his imperfections.

Still feeling the effects of the liquor, Jana thought about that portrait of Ed she'd promised the first day back from Yaddo. Maybe she'd superimpose the lion's head on Ed's. His eyes would be large and unfocused, as they always were without his contacts in. He would be bearded, and his hair would be yellow, not white. Or brown, rather—real lions had brown manes, even if Leroy's was the same yellow as the rest of his body. She'd suggested Ed grow a beard once, and he'd scoffed at the idea, insisting they were dirty and unmanageable—but who knows, anything's possible. Laughing at their unlimited possibilities, she turned toward him again, kissing the back of his neck. His neck was always as smooth as if he'd shaved it, cool to the touch no matter how warm the rest of his body was.